Praise for *In Plain Sight*

"I loved this YA Christian romantic mystery/adventure. Expertly meshing mystery, suspense, romance, (and secret passages!), Leslea Wahl's *In Plain Sight* is a page turner with spot-on pacing and heroic characters. Emerson finds herself suddenly in a new world: cold, dark, remote Minnesota. As Wahl tantalizingly dangles cryptic memories of the teen's past, the reader is kept guessing at why she and her dad are living on their own in this bleak landscape. Adding to the charm of the characters, and to my delight, Emerson's dog, Zuri, brings a dose of fun and real life to the story with his antics. (I vividly imagined the daily struggle of getting booties off and on the reluctant dog's paws!) Get ready for some twists and turns, swoony moments, and, if you've read the other books in this series, the return of some familiar faces. I can't wait to share this latest in the Finding Faith series with my teenage daughters." ~ Carolyn Astfalk, author of *Ornamental Graces*; past president of the Catholic Writers Guild

"When it comes to books for teens that are a blend of mystery and sweet romance, Leslea Wahl is in a league of her own. *In Plain Sight* is a captivating story revolving around sixteen-year-old Emerson, who has been forced to move to the frozen Midwest with her father after a tragedy occurs in their family. Wahl does an outstanding job of creating true-to-life teen characters who have strengths and weaknesses, who've done things they regret, and yet are striving to be better versions of themselves every day. Her depiction of first love will resonate with readers of all ages. Whether you are a teen now or were a teen at some point in your life, this book is for you." ~ Amanda Lauer, author of the award-winning Heaven Intended Series

"Leslea Wahl delivers again with another gripping, fast-paced novel that combines a spell-binding plot, sweet romance, intrigue, and the powerful love of family. *In Plain Sight* is a page-turner which will leave you wishing for more." ~ Andrea Jo Rodgers, author of *Heaven-Sent Miracles and Rescues*

Other Titles by Leslea Wahl

The Perfect Blindside
eXtreme Blindside
Where You Lead
Into the Spotlight
Charting the Course
To Serve and Protect
The Mommy Mix-up

Contributing author in CatholicTeenBooks anthologies:

Secrets: Visible & Invisible
Gifts: Visible & Invisible
Treasures: Visible & Invisible
Ashes: Visible & Invisible
Shadows: Visible & Invisible

In Plain Sight

Finding Faith, Book 3

LESLEA WAHL

Chapter 1

As we drive further into the frozen, barren landscape, I slowly begin to embrace the gray desolation of my new home. This lifeless terrain is a fitting punishment and matches my inner turmoil to perfection. Everything good and beautiful in my life is gone, leaving me with this unyielding, bitter iciness that surrounds me.

Dad slows the truck. "Well, Em, looks like we're almost there."

I turn from looking out the frosted side window but see no signs of life, so I glance at the GPS map. Aside from the road we've been traveling, we've seen nothing for miles. But, sure enough, one single line snakes off from our current path.

He slowly makes the turn, and suddenly we're swallowed by a thick, dark forest where anything could lurk. The tires crunch across hard-packed snow. Our change in speed signals Zuri to pop her head up. Everyone thinks my black dog is a lab. She's actually a shepherd mix and a fabulous family pet. Lately, she has advanced in status to that of a much-needed, faithful companion.

In the dark, unfamiliar surroundings, she lets out a prolonged whine. I reach back and pat her head. She seems as unnerved as I am by the towering snowbanks that line the sides of the road. Leaning forward on the console between Dad and me, she peers out the front window. In this winter wonderland, the white starburst of fur on her chest might easily be a snowflake.

Tall, snow-covered pines create long purple shadows, adding to the already eerie effect of surroundings that would be the perfect setting for a horror movie—the desolation, the hopelessness, the foreboding.

The trees begin to thin out, and Dad eases up on the gas. He stops the truck next to a pretty log home with a wraparound porch. A welcoming plume of smoke billows from the stone chimney—probably the only inviting thing for miles.

After switching off the ignition, Dad leans back in his seat and lets out a low whistle as he takes in the scene. On our right, a frozen lake is surrounded by a forest of tall pines, each with a dusting of fresh snow. Further down the lane from where we're parked, a white lodge looks out over the water from a spot at its edge. The place appears to be a small, two-story hotel with probably no more than twenty guest rooms. Even from this distance, it's clear a little TLC would be a good thing. Paint has peeled away in large areas on the exterior walls. Missing tiles have left jagged voids on the roof. Several shutters hang askew, rather like a massive beast shedding its winter coat. But a large gazebo at the water's edge hints at the charm the lodge once portrayed. Scattered behind the main building, several small cabins appear as sad and neglected as the main lodge. Dad has his work cut out for him.

He turns and looks at me. His grin doesn't hide the lines of fatigue and worry. "Welcome to O'Malley Lake, kid. Ready for our next adventure?"

I attempt a small smile but am unable to coerce any kind of sincerity, though I reach to the depths of my soul. It's certainly not his fault that our life has crumbled to pieces, and I shouldn't take my misery out on him. With my smile a total bust, I give him a thumbs-up. "Ready as I'll ever be."

I open the car door, and an onslaught of the coldest air I've ever known seems bent on snatching my breath. A shocked gasp fills my lungs with unbearably icy cold. I slam the door shut to block out the elements.

With a chuckle, Dad reaches into the back seat for my jacket and tosses it at me. "Welcome to Minnesota in January."

With a huff, I slip on the coat, then gloves and hat from my pockets. I pull the knit hat over my blonde hair before trying to exit the truck once again. However, the added layers do little to warm me up. In moments, I'm unable to feel my cheeks, which are already numb from the cold. Who in their right mind moves to Minnesota in the middle of winter?

Easy. Those who have no choice.

I'm about to give up on this venture and retreat to the warmth of the truck when a man exits the log house and tromps toward us. The steam trailing from a mug in his bare hand is the most inviting thing I've seen all day.

In a few long strides, the tall, broad-shouldered man reaches us. The hand not holding a hot mug slides from his jacket pocket and extends toward Dad. "Mr. Harris?"

Dad offers his gloved hand for the shake. "Call me Brad. And you must be Mitch Stevenson."

Strands of gray highlight Mr. Stevenson's dark hair, making him appear to be about Dad's age. He nods and then offers me a welcoming smile. "You must be Emerson."

My teeth chatter in response, while Zuri lets out a friendly bark from the truck.

Mr. Stevenson motions for us to follow him. "Come on, let's get you inside."

I return to the truck and yank open the passenger door so Zuri can leap out. Instead of staying near me as she usually does, she sprints toward the porch of the log cabin. I can't blame her. Her poor paws must be freezing. Somewhere in our belongings are the booties and matching sweater I bought her. And I'd thought Dad was crazy when he suggested them. A surge of envy at Zuri's speed fills my every cell as the bitter cold prevents me from doing anything but stiffly follow along. Why would people choose to live here?

The cozy home is even more inviting inside. A roaring fire in the beautiful stone fireplace immediately draws Zuri and me closer. As I thaw out, I scan the photos on the log mantle. Most of them are of a family of four. Mr. Stevenson is easily recognizable, so I assume the other three people are his wife and two children—a boy and a girl. The most recent photo is of a lanky middle-school boy and an elementary-aged girl. Judging by the backgrounds of the pictures, the family enjoys hiking and camping.

"Please make yourselves at home." Mr. Stevenson slips out of his jacket. The sleeves of his plaid shirt are rolled up, revealing muscular forearms. He probably stays fit by chopping logs to keep the fireplace stocked all winter so they don't freeze to death.

A petite woman with wavy auburn hair appears with a tray of mugs. Mrs. Stevenson, I presume. Her diminutive stature makes her husband look even more solid and brawny. "I heated up some cider." She sets the tray on a wooden coffee table. "I'm Diedre, Dee for short. Mitch and I are so thrilled that you're here." She offers me a mug. "Hopefully, you didn't have any trouble on the journey." Her sweet smile reminds me so much of Mom that I have to avert my gaze and blink away tears.

I wrap my hands around the mug. The cinnamon-apple scent wafts up in a cloud of steam even as welcoming heat seeps through my gloves. Maybe I won't lose my fingers to frostbite, after all. At least, not today. "Thank you. This is wonderful."

The men make themselves comfortable in leather armchairs, and Dee sits on the couch amid an abundance of decorative pillows. Finally, having stopped shivering, I set down my mug and peel off the layers that seem woefully inadequate for the climate of our new state.

While the adults chat, I pick up my mug and scan the room, impressed with Dee's knack for decorating. She's combined rugged, woodsy pieces with modern items to create a welcoming, elegant atmosphere.

"You have a beautiful piece of property here." Dad looks out the large picture window toward the frozen lake.

Dee reaches for her husband's hand. "It's always been Mitch's dream to live on a lake."

Mitch's lopsided grin is endearing. "And Dee has always wanted to run a bed and breakfast, so this seemed like the perfect combination."

Dee releases her husband's hand and tucks her legs beneath her. "I'm envisioning more of a special event center for weddings, family reunions, and retreats. But, as you can tell by the state of the lodge, we have some work to do in order to make that vision a reality."

Dad faces the Stevensons and takes a sip of his cider. "And that's where I come in."

Mitch nods. "Yes, we're hoping you'll be able to help us get the old place in usable shape by the time spring rolls around."

Dad's eyes narrow as he peers out the giant picture window toward the lodge. "I'll do my best." He turns his attention to his new employer. "Thank you for this opportunity."

As the men discuss the details, Dee offers me another welcoming smile. "Emerson, will you be attending Lake Forest High School?"

I shake my head and sit down next to her. "No. I'll be finishing the year online."

She nods slowly. Her penetrating gaze forces me to look down at the amber-colored cider. "This is really good, by the way."

"It's an old family recipe," she says. "We fixed up one of the cabins for you and your dad. I think you'll be comfortable there. If you're ready to brave the cold again, I could show it to you."

I'm most definitely not ready to venture outside so soon after thawing out, but I don't want to be rude, so I drain the rest of the warm liquid, raising my internal temperature. "Sounds great."

After bundling up, I follow Dee down the lane toward the cabins, Zuri at our heels. My hostess stops at the nearest building— a little log cabin with a cute front porch. It's smaller than where she and her family live, but it's an adequate size for just Dad and me. Dee opens the front door, and I follow her into the toasty living room. A fire has already been lit in the stone fireplace, a smaller version of the one at the Stevenson's home.

"Feel free to take down any of these decorations and put up your own," Dee says as I glance around at the woodland décor.

I gaze at the bear and elk knick-knacks. "They're great. We didn't really bring much with us."

A curious Zuri leads the tour, taking us through the living room and into the kitchen—not large, but it'll do the trick.

She points toward the fridge. "I wasn't sure how much you or your dad liked to cook, so I stocked your freezer with a few meals. We also bought some essentials for the fridge and cupboards."

I drop my gloves on the small kitchen table. "That's so kind. I hadn't even thought of any of that yet."

Dee leads me across the living room to the two bedrooms. I'm thankful to see each comes with its own bathroom. Not having to share one with Dad will be a nice change. Each room is furnished with a queen-sized bed covered by a patchwork quilt and numerous pillows. The bedframes are made of pine logs and fit the woodland theme perfectly. Patterned rugs add color to the wood floors and will help eliminate the click-clacky noise of Zuri's toenails as she walks.

I smile at Dee. "Thanks. This is perfect."

She clasps her hands in front of her. "If you think of anything else you need, let me know."

I swallow the lump in my throat, a bit overwhelmed by her thoughtfulness.

She reaches out and gently touches my hand. "Emerson, please come by the house at any time, for any reason. While I was excited to purchase this place, I didn't realize how isolated we would be—especially at this time of year. It's truly wonderful to have you here. I'm sure Reid and Raina will also be thrilled. They get tired of just having their mom and dad around." She again offers me the caring smile that reminds me so much of Mom.

"I look forward to meeting your kids."

She looks around. "Well, I'll let you get settled. Mitch and your dad will bring your things in soon." She gives Zuri a goodbye pat and leaves.

I look out the front window toward the lake and the sad-looking lodge, trying to imagine how it might have looked "once upon a time." Dad's a fantastic contractor. If anyone can return this place to its original splendor, he can.

If only he could work that same magic on our shattered lives.

Chapter 2

"Okay, ready to explore?"

Zuri wags her tail in reply to my query, anxious for a more energetic activity after spending most of the day cooped up in our cabin while I labored over my schoolwork. One benefit of online classes is how quickly I can get through all my subjects. I plowed through the work, ate a bowl of leftover stew, and am now ready for a change of scenery.

However, the simple plan of going outside proves easier said than done. While I know Zuri will benefit from the booties designed to protect her delicate paws from the icy cold, she has made her disdain for the paw-wear evident. She keeps attempting to fling them off, making the process more difficult than it should be. When I come after her with the sweater, she engages in a game—a mix of hide-and-seek and chase. By the time I finally have her dressed for the weather, I'm sweating and have no desire to put on more layers. But knowing my elevated core temp won't last long, I proceed to don boots, gloves, hat, coat, and scarf.

Feeling like the Abominable Snow Monster, I peer down at Zuri, who has finally resigned herself to the new accoutrements. "Let's do this."

She springs to her feet, her annoyance at me and the despised booties instantly evaporating.

I brace myself before pulling open the door of our cabin. My eyes squeeze shut in response to the blast of frigid air. Will I ever get used to this?

Zuri leads the way, looking like a show horse. She gingerly lifts her paws high in the air as she walks, acclimating to her new footwear. I wait on the porch as she sniffs a few trees and takes care of business. Then she looks at me with her big brown eyes, and I point my mittened hand toward the lodge. She lets out a bark and races down the shoveled pathway toward the looming building. By the time I reach her, we are both shivering.

The side door Mr. Stevenson told me to use opens to a long, shadowy hallway. I listen for him and my dad. Have they finished their tour of the lodge? Their plan for the day was to go room by room, making a list of all the needed repairs. While I'm not a contractor like Dad, a simple look at the place makes me suspect it will be a very long list.

Zuri and I make our way past peeling paint, worn carpet, and piles of debris. I can't help but wonder about Mr. and Mrs. Stevenson's judgment. This place is a dump.

The dark hallway brightens as we move toward the center of the lodge, opening up to a pleasant surprise. Sunlight penetrates the grungy windows, highlighting a two-story lobby. Maybe I judged the Stevensons too quickly.

A huge antler chandelier hangs in the middle of the space, suspended high above the wide planks of dark wood. I wander toward the oversized front doors and peer out the grimy glass at a blanket of snow. Remnants of a wooden railing peek out above the white powder in various spots. We'll have to wait until the snow melts to be sure, but I'm guessing an expansive deck is buried beneath the mound of white, and possibly even stairs leading down to a driveway and parking lot.

Turning, I pretend to be a visitor, entering the lodge for the first time. I imagine how the welcoming space once might've looked. To my left is a large, wooden check-in counter where a friendly clerk would have greeted their newest guest. To the right, an elegant staircase leads to the second floor. An eager bellhop may have carried my luggage to my room. While the upper floor is definitely a place to explore at some point, what lies directly ahead of me intrigues me far more.

Lured by the view, I walk toward the wall of smudged glass windows and double doors in the next room. The trim on all of them is white, adding the perfect frame to the *piéce de résistance*—O'Malley Lake.

Today, the sun shines brightly, and the frozen lake sparkles, creating a field of radiant diamonds. Breathtaking. Almost beautiful enough to make me forget my sorrows.

I force my gaze off the icy scene to check out the room. This must be the dining hall. The walls are painted a pale seafoam green with white trim. A few white tables and chairs have been pushed against the back wall. A set of swinging doors on the right side of the dining room most likely lead to the kitchen.

I look to my left, where warm tones beckon from the next room. Zuri dutifully pads along beside me. While she sniffs all the nooks and crannies, I admire the beauty of this new space, which might be described as a library or a parlor. Either way, I'm awed by the dark wood, floor-to-ceiling bookshelves, and bay windows with plush, maroon cushions. Mom would love it here. The thought pulls me from the brief moment of enjoyment, because the stark reality is that neither she nor the twins will ever see this place.

"Oh, there you are!"

I jump and spin toward the voice behind me.

"Oops…sorry. I didn't mean to scare you." A girl with long brown hair bends down to pet Zuri, who's wagging her tail so hard her whole back end wiggles from the movement. "What's your name, sweet puppy?"

I step toward the girl, who I'm guessing is in middle school. "That's Zuri. I'm Em, short for Emerson."

The girl's smile reveals a mouthful of metal. "I'm so glad to finally meet you. I'm Raina." Then she calls over her shoulder. "Reid, get in here. I found her."

Through the doorway walks a vision—a tall teenage boy with a warm grin that just might melt that frozen lake. His brown eyes are a few shades darker than the hazel color I inherited from my dad. In my previous life—back when things like that seemed important—he would've been just my type.

Our eyes briefly lock before he strides forward, running a hand through thick, dark hair. "Hey. Sorry to barge in on you. Raina couldn't wait a moment longer. She's been so excited to meet you."

Still wearing her sweater and booties, Zuri pads over to check him out.

After a moment, I realize I'm staring, and avert my gaze. "Sorry. I saw your pictures at your home, but I thought—I mean, the photos must be a few years old."

Reid laughs. "Yeah, we keep telling Mom she needs to update the mantle photos, but she's too sentimental to remove the old ones. If you wander farther into the house, you'll see plenty of recent ones."

"Our pictures seem to be her favorite decoration," Raina adds. "Have you looked around the rest of this place?"

I shake my head. "No, not yet."

Her eyes light up. "Come on, we'll show you."

She and Zuri scurry from the room. I glance at Reid, who's shaking his head in amusement.

"Like I said, my sister has been eager for your arrival."

I give him a nod, not sure how to respond. I'm surprised someone was happy that we were coming here, because I sure wasn't. "Well, a tour would be great."

Reid leads the way to the lobby. Raina and Zuri are sitting on the bottom step of the grand staircase. Zuri's holding one paw in midair—a plea for her new friend to remove the dreaded paw-wear. They both look at me with matching pleading eyes.

I cave. "I guess her paws are warm enough in here."

Raina beams a silvery smile and removes the first bootie, earning herself a slobbery kiss.

"So, how long has your family owned this place?" I try to fill the time while Reid and I wait for the unshackling.

He looks around the open area. "About six months. Dad was searching for a new venture, and Mom thought this would be a great way to get out of the city but still bring in some income."

Finished with her task, Raina places the four canine booties in a neat pile beside her and then stands. "And I think they didn't want to uproot us again."

I follow Raina and Zuri up the wooden staircase. "You've moved around a lot?" My last dreadful housing arrangement comes to mind.

"All the time," she says over her shoulder. "Dad was in the military when we were younger."

Military. That would explain Mr. Stevenson's muscular build.

"He still does some consulting work," Reid adds.

Reaching the second-floor landing, I nod as I take in the worn and stained red carpet that lines the long hallway in both directions. Raina turns left and begins the tour through the different guest rooms, each in various forms of disrepair. The lodge has obviously been neglected for some time.

"Do you know much about this place?" I peer out one of the windows toward the frozen lake and dark forest.

Reid leans against the door frame. "The original structure was first built in 1912. There have been some additions since then. We hear that a lot of lake lodges were used as summer getaways for city folks. Before air conditioning, it was nice to escape to the woods, I guess. The land was homesteaded in the 1800s, and for most of the time since then, it belonged to one family. More recently, a few different organizations owned it."

Raina smacks her brother's arm, and he flinches. "You make it sound boring. You didn't mention anything about the mysterious deaths, the reported ghost sightings, or the hidden room."

My eyes widen. "Are you serious?"

Before either of them can answer, our fathers appear in the doorway, both covered in dirt. Their inspection had clearly been thorough.

"I'm glad to see you're getting the grand tour." Mr. Stevenson gives me a broad smile.

Raina approaches my dad. "Well, what do you think? Will you be able to help us get this place back in order?"

Dad grins at her. "I'm confident it can be restored to its former glory. Luckily, it's got good bones."

Mr. Stevenson pulls out his phone. He scans a text, then his gaze travels between Dad and me. "My lovely wife wants me to invite you both for dinner."

"That would be awesome!" Raina squeals. "And Zuri, too."

Dad glances at me, and I shrug a shoulder in response. Even though I've had about as much polite conversation and human contact as I can handle for one day, the thought of preparing dinner, even if it's just warming up one of Mrs. Stevenson's readymade meals, sounds overwhelming.

Dad seems to understand my complex array of emotions. He looks back at his new employer. "That sounds wonderful, and we promise we won't overstay our welcome. Let me freshen up, and then we'll be over."

~

The moment Dad and I sit down for dinner with the Stevensons, I know we've made a mistake. The steaming casserole looks and smells tantalizingly delicious, and my stomach rumbles in response. Yet it also fills me with melancholy. This is precisely the type of meal Mom used to make. I mumble my way through the dinner blessing—something Dad and I haven't said in recent months. Our old traditions are just too painful to continue.

The meal passes pleasantly enough as the adults discuss the lodge, and Raina shares about something that happened at school. Reid remains nearly as quiet as I do, making my lack of social skills less obvious. Let them think I'm a brooding teen. Who cares?

After dinner, Raina disappears, saying she wants to teach Zuri a trick. Reid and I help Mrs. Stevenson with the dishes as the men move to the living room to continue their riveting discussion of drywall and plumbing fixtures.

"Thank you so much for dinner. It was delicious." I address Mrs. Stevenson as I set a pile of dishes in the sink.

"You are very welcome, Em." She smiles as she transfers the remaining casserole into a plastic container. "I enjoy cooking, so you and your dad are welcome at our table anytime."

Reid grins. "Dad says her love language is cooking."

"Well, lucky me!" I grin back. "I don't really know much about cooking. That was always my mom's job." I clamp my mouth shut, keeping my emotions from escaping.

Mrs. Stevenson's smile brims with compassion. "Well, please join us at any time."

"Thank you." I'm thinking of a way to change the topic when her gaze darts toward the living room.

"Mom, I know you want to hear what they're discussing about the lodge. We can take care of the rest of this." Reid waves his mother to the door.

Her face scrunches as she considers his offer. "I would hate for them to make any decisions that don't align with my vision for the place."

"Reid's right. We've got this." I try to assure her, even though I'm leery about being alone with her son. Talking to cute boys has never been my strong suit. Add to that the fact that my social skills are a little rusty, and the task becomes downright precarious.

"Okay. Thank you." She squeezes my arm and leaves the room.

Reid looks at me. "Sorry to force you into chores, but I know how much she wants to be part of every decision with the lodge."

"Makes sense."

He turns on the sink faucet, adjusting the handle until he's satisfied with the water temperature. "How about I rinse, and you load?"

"Deal." I pull the dishwasher door open. "Do you like living out here in the woods?"

"Yeah, it's cool. It's a little far from school and friends, though." He hands me a plate. "I have to drive Raina to school now, which isn't the coolest thing to do, but it's not bad." He shoots me that cute grin of his.

I strategically place the plate on the bottom rack as I try to think of something else to talk about.

"My turn to ask a question." He comes to my rescue. "Mom said you're taking online classes instead of going to Lake Forest High?"

I nod, taking the glass he offers me. "Since we moved partway through the semester, I thought it might be easier for now."

"Well, if you ever want to meet people, let me know. You could go with me to one of the school sporting events or my youth group."

"Thanks, I'll keep that in mind." Would we be here long enough to actually make friends? "Is Lake Forest the closest town?"

Reid hands me another plate. "No, but it's the largest in the area. It's about fifteen minutes south of here. But if you head down our lane and continue north on the main road, you'll come across a small town called Hermann. There's not much there, though. A little grocery store, a hardware store, a library with a coffee shop, and a couple churches."

An unnerving silence fills the room until a new topic finally pops into mind. "Hey, Raina mentioned a hidden room in the lodge. What's up with that?"

Reid shoots me a sly smile. "Ahh, intrigued by our little mystery?"

My cheeks warm. "Mysteries are always intriguing." Although, as I know all too well, they also can lead to downfall.

Reid looks at me for a moment, like he's considering something. Then he reaches for a dishtowel and dries his hands. "Want to meet me at the lodge tomorrow when I get home from school? I'll show you what Raina and I discovered."

"Sounds great." My smile—genuine, if a little rusty—comes easy as a twinge of interest zips through me. I haven't experienced anything even close to this kind of curiosity in months. It's good to know I still can.

Chapter 3

I've lived in a sort of suspended reality ever since my world came undone…unaware of the passage of time. So today's constant glancing at the clock is unexpected. How long has it been since I've had something to look forward to?

The day's task of schoolwork, a brief walk with Zuri, and a few mundane chores do little to help speed things up. But eventually, the three o'clock hour arrives, and I sit in the rocking chair near the window to watch for Reid's SUV. The rug beneath the chair takes the brunt of my built-up energy as I rock wildly back and forth.

My wait is short. Reid's dark green vehicle slowly nears his house, causing a nervous flutter inside me. What am I thinking? It's been so long since I've interacted with anyone other than my dad that I'm no longer confident in my interpersonal skills. At least this time we won't be alone, which eases some of the pressure. Raina has no trouble keeping a conversation going all by herself. And Zuri's always a good distraction.

As I commence the bundling-up process, Zuri stretches and wags her tail.

"Okay, are we ready for this?" I hold up her sweater and booties. She whines but acquiesces, and I'm able to dress her in record time.

Finally ready, I open the door and Zuri bounds outside, sprinting toward Reid, who is walking toward our cabin. He stops and crouches down to pet her, his winter gloves stroking her shiny black fur. Then he looks up, smiles, and waves at me with his free hand.

I wrap my arms around myself, my boots crunching across the hard snow. "Hi! Where's Raina?"

Reid stands. "She has a piano lesson this afternoon."

"Oh." It's just Reid and me? No energetic Raina to keep the dialogue flowing? Is there a way to put this off? Doubtful. Since I have no life, absolutely no reasonable excuse exists not to do this. He would know I didn't want to be alone with him, and that would be totally embarrassing. Better to suck it up and go.

"Shall we?" Reid gestures toward the lodge.

"Yes, please, before I lose my toes." And my nerve.

He laughs as he starts walking. "Not used to the cold?"

"Does anyone ever get used to it?"

"I had assumed you were from around here."

I shake my head, conserving my words as the cold burns my lungs each time I speak. But since he's walking ahead of me and doesn't have eyes in the back of his head, I'm forced to answer. "We've also moved around a bit. Most recently, we were in Arizona."

He looks back at me. "Really? Yeah, this would be harsh after living in the desert. Phoenix?" He reaches the side door and holds it open for Zuri and me.

I quickly enter the building and stomp the snow off my boots. "No, Flagstaff. It actually snows there, but it's not nearly this frigid."

We make our way toward the lobby.

"How long did you live there?" Does he really want to know, or is Reid also looking for something to keep the conversation going?

"A while." I'm deliberately vague.

Thankfully, he doesn't press for a more concrete answer. "Where were you before that?"

"Various Midwest cities." Time to change the subject. "Enough about me. I'm dying to know more about this hidden room."

We reach the large lobby area, and I'm finally able to pull off the knit hat and unloop my scarf. Since the Stevensons don't want to waste energy heating up the entire lodge—a completely logical decision—the place is uncomfortably chilly. Dad plans on moving portable heaters around to whatever room he's working on.

Zuri watches me peel away the layers, then flicks her paw until one of her booties flies free.

Reid raises an eyebrow. "I'm not sure she's a fan of those things." He retrieves it for me.

"She has a short memory. You should have seen the drama queen when I let her out this morning without the booties. Within less than thirty seconds, she started marching like a robot, trying to keep her paws out of the snow."

He laughs at my description.

"Back to the subject at hand…the hidden room." I know I've got a one-track mind, but that's who I am. Plus, I'm so glad to actually be tingling with interest in anything, I just can't let it go.

He grins. "Right. A woman on a mission. I like it. Right this way."

Is he making fun of me? I wince. *He's probably wishing he never suggested this outing.*

I follow him into the library, where I first met him and Raina. My favorite room is just as enticing as it was before. Despite the dark wooden panels and bookshelves, the space remains bright, thanks to the light bursting through the tall windows that face the lake.

As it did yesterday, the room fills me with wonder and peace. I close my eyes and take a deep breath as I picture guests browsing the shelves, searching for a new adventure. Happy with their selections, they curl up in comfy chairs or lounge on the window seats, ready to get lost in a grand story. Suddenly aware of my daydreaming, I pop open my eyes.

Reid stands before me, his expression unreadable.

Heat rushes like a volcano from somewhere near my tummy to settle in my cheeks like a flashing marquee. I knew interacting with humans was a bad idea.

A true gentleman, Reid pretends my odd behavior is totally normal. "This place is pretty magical, isn't it?"

I nod. "It's beautiful, and so inviting."

"I know what you mean. Raina and I have both been drawn to this part of the lodge. We spent a good part of the summer here. That's how we found the hidden room." He walks past the impressive fireplace and the bookshelves to the far wall. Once there, he presses on a section of the dark wood paneling until there is an audible click.

He swings back toward me, his eyes filled with mischief. With one hand, he pushes on the wall, and it slides open, revealing another room.

"Whoa." I look at him with wide eyes. "This is amazing."

I move closer to peer into the dark space, expecting a dim, dusty corridor. But when Reid flips a switch, I find myself looking at a spacious room. Beneath the layers of dust, I'm sure the place is as warm and inviting as the library. A large pool table takes up the center of the space, with colored billiard balls and cue sticks resting on maroon felt. On the left side of the room, an old-fashioned bar runs the entire length of the wall. I walk closer, peering at the bottles of colored liquid lined up in front of a large mirror.

Nearby, a high-top table is piled with items. Books, two glasses, and an ashtray with a half-smoked cigar…like some party was interrupted and never restarted. Everything is coated in a thick layer of dust.

"Was this created during Prohibition?" It seems a logical reason for a hidden bar. I turn to Reid with the question.

He shrugs. "We're not sure. Either that, or maybe the men just wanted their own space."

I shoot him a scolding look. "Or the women banished them from the more refined area."

He laughs. "An early man-cave of sorts."

That's when a familiar twinge of excitement takes over again. My curiosity has been piqued, and there's no turning back. "Do you think this house holds more secrets?"

His eyes narrow as he considers my words. "Maybe. I mean, it's possible."

I run my hand along the long-forgotten pool table, leaving a trail through the layers of dust. Maybe life here won't be so boring here, after all.

Maybe I'll actually *have* a life.

Chapter 4

I set the table for dinner, my mind drifting back to the hidden room. Too bad Reid had to leave to pick up Raina before I could discover more of the lodge's secrets. Oh, well. There will be plenty of time for that during the long, cold winter that lies ahead. I set down the last of the silverware just as Dad whisks through the back door, along with a burst of cold air. He stomps his boots on the rug, knocking off clumps of snow. Zuri rushes over to greet him.

"It smells delicious in here." He offers a smile as he slips out of his coat.

"Mrs. Stevenson to the rescue again." Appalled, I watch him peel off his winter gear. He's streaked with smears of dirt from his forehead to the hem of his dirty jeans. His dark hair is practically white from the dust that covers it. My mouth drops open. I'm not sure there's a clean spot on him. "You look like you've been mauled by a flock of angry Canadian geese."

He glances down at his filthy work shirt. Somewhere through the course of the day it had transformed from pale green to a camo print. "I spent most of the day in airducts and crawl spaces."

I point toward the bedrooms. "You need a shower before we eat."

He grins and snaps a salute. "Yes, ma'am."

While he cleans up, I pull the bubbling casserole out of the oven to let it cool and place a few slices of what looks like home-made bread on a plate. After I set the food on the table, I realize this is the first time I've ever prepared dinner completely on my own. I'd spent far too much of the last few months hidden away in my room, okay with Dad taking the lead on anything domestic. But now that he'll be working so hard on the lodge, it's my turn to step up.

"So, how was your day, kid?" Dad asks as he enters the kitchen looking much better in clean jeans and a flannel shirt. The few gray strands in his damp, dark hair gleam from the bright over-head light.

"Pretty good." I sit down while Dad scoops himself an extra-large helping of the casserole.

"What do you think of the lodge?" I ask. "Do you think you can get it back in shape by spring, like they're hoping?"

"Yes. Although it's a big project." He glances at me. "If I see the job through to its completion, we could be here a while."

I center my attention on dishing myself a much smaller help-ing.

When I don't respond, he adds, "We'll just see how it goes."

"It's not the worst place in the world...except for the cold." I take a bite of the delicious, creamy casserole.

He laughs. "Yeah, the chill factor is a bit much, isn't it? But it doesn't seem to stop these Minnesotans." He adds a spoonful of mixed veggies to his plate. "The Stevensons want me to start on the lodge's dining room. Apparently, Reid has invited some of his friends over for an ice-skating party on the lake, and they'll need somewhere warm to congregate afterwards."

I shiver just thinking about being outdoors for an extended period of time.

"Did you and Zuri do anything fun today?"

Zuri's ears perk up at the mention of her name.

"Actually, Reid played tour guide again." I watch his face, wanting to see his reaction to the question I'm about to ask. "Hey, did you know about the secret room?"

He cocks an eyebrow at me. "The one off the library?"

I set my fork down. "Do you think there's more than one?"

He shrugs. "Possibly. Hidden spaces aren't unheard of in these older buildings."

"Really? Why?"

He reaches for one of the slices of bread. "That often depends on the age of the building. If it was built in the mid-1800s, there might have been hidden rooms to hide runaway slaves. If it was built in the '20s, the owner could've been hiding a speakeasy or something. Sometimes, lodge owners had passageways built simply for staff to use so they could go about unnoticed. Or the rooms could have been built just for the novelty of it. That's what the pool room appears to be."

"That's cool." I contemplate the different scenarios and wonder if there's a way to figure out more about this particular hidden room.

"Or maybe it was something more sinister." When I look up from my plate, he wiggles his eyebrows at me. "I know of one famous case of a serial killer creating hidden rooms in a hotel in Chicago during the World's Fair as a place to imprison his victims."

"This place seems too sweet and wholesome to have been used for something evil."

"I agree. No creepy vibes emanating from this building."

Or were there? Raina had mentioned something about a mysterious death. That old lodge probably holds a lot of secrets. Researching the history of this place could fill up some of my time, and prove a nice distraction.

Dad interrupts my thoughts. "Hey, I need to drive to Minneapolis tomorrow to place an order and pick up some supplies. Since it's Saturday, want to come along?"

"Sorry, but hanging out in building supply stores doesn't exactly sound fun."

He grins. "I thought I could drop you off at the Mall of America before I run my errands. I'm told it's the largest mall in the U.S."

While the idea is somewhat appealing, I'm afraid it might make me sad that I can't experience it with Mom or my sisters. "Maybe another time. I was actually thinking of spending some time in the library at the lodge." Ever since I saw that room, I've been longing to curl up there with a good book.

He looks a little disappointed but nods anyway. "Those portable heaters Mr. Stevenson purchased work great. One of them should keep you toasty warm."

"Perfect. As much as I like my parka, it would be nice not to have to wear it all day."

He grins and then clears his throat. "I'll pick up a pizza on the way home. Maybe we can have a movie night," he says tentatively. "You can even pick the film."

A movie night with just the two of us? Sounds lonely. Pretending everything is normal is tiresome. I swirl my fork through my food and try to force some lightness to my voice. "Sure, that would be fun."

Chapter 5

I wake the next morning to Zuri bopping me with her paw. My left eye peels open. Her face is a blurry blob, mere inches from mine. "Morning, girl."

Her tail taps out an excited rhythm against my wooden bed frame. I push back the patchwork quilt, lured to the kitchen by the tantalizing smell of bacon. A covered pan rests on the stovetop, and a saltshaker holds a note in place on the table. I pick it up and read Dad's messy scrawl.

Didn't want to wake you. Not sure how long I'll be gone. You mentioned you might go over to the lodge. Left something for you in the library.

I devour the bacon and eggs, then get ready for the day. After searching through a few kitchen cupboards, I find a thermos and some hot cocoa packets. Perfect for a day of reading.

Zuri squirms even less today as I dress her in her winter attire. Then, with both of us bundled to face the elements, we leave the cabin.

A fine layer of snow blankets our previous day's footprints. Zuri buries her nose in the white fluff, intrigued with some new scent. I keep moving, and she soon bounds after me, catching up with a few long strides, her black snout now powdered in snow.

I pull open the side door of the lodge, and Zuri sprints down the hallway toward the library, somehow knowing that's where I'm headed. When I finally join her, she's sitting in the middle of the room, patiently waiting.

I pat her head. "You're so smart."

Glancing around the room, I search for Dad's surprise. I'm assuming he set up one of the portable heaters for me, but I'm wrong. Instead, he's provided an even better heating alternative. One of those easy-burn logs waits in the fireplace. A lighter and a few real logs sit on the hearth. I smile. This day is getting better by the moment.

Soon, we're unbundled, and Zuri curls up on the rug in front of the stone fireplace where orange flames perform a hypnotic dance. As the room begins to warm, I scan the shelves of hardcover classics. Knickknacks add interest to the rows of books. I finally decide on *Persuasion*, a Jane Austen book I've yet to read. After pouring myself a cup of cocoa, I tentatively sink into the red velvet couch, half expecting the fabric to rip, or an errant spring to poke me. But the piece of furniture is surprisingly comfortable.

As I settle in, enjoying the rare moment of contentment, I once again admire the picture-perfect setting, with the glowing fireplace and beautiful, dark wood shelves. However, the longer I stare at the shelves, the more distracted I become. Something seems off, but I can't pinpoint what's wrong. Maybe it's the weird busts of the old geezers watching me with their piercing eyes, scrutinizing my complicated past.

I glance from one to the other. "I'm counting on you two to keep my secrets quiet."

Zuri's head pops up, assuming I'm talking to her. I shake my head and open the book. Talking to inanimate objects is probably not a good sign for the status of my mental health.

Getting into the old-fashioned, formal-style English writing takes a minute or two, but soon, I lose track of time as I'm completely immersed in the story.

The squeaky opening of the side door breaks the peaceful silence. A barking Zuri dashes out of the room. My growling stomach informs me I've been reading for quite a while.

Reid's voice greets Zuri, bringing a smile to my face. I sit up, ready to greet him, when a female voice I don't recognize begins oohing and aahing about Zuri's cuteness. He's not alone, and that causes a surprising twinge of disappointment. I set down my book and stand, just as four teens enter the room. Alongside Reid is a tall guy with a lopsided grin and two pretty girls who look around my age.

"Hey, Emerson." Reid smiles in greeting. "Sorry to disturb you. I didn't realize you were here."

Before I remind him that he has nothing to apologize for since it's his property, not mine, the girl with the light brown hair flowing from her knit hat squats down next to Zuri. "Your dog is so sweet. Reid says her name is Zuri?"

I watch Zuri roll on her back, offering her tummy for a rub. "Yep, that's right."

"Oh, you are adorable, Miss Zuri." The girl coos in a high-pitched voice, eliciting an all-over, joyful wiggle from my dog. "Oh!" The girl looks at me. "*Miss Zuri* sounds like the state—Missouri!"

"No!" I'm not the only one startled by the snap in my tone. They all turn wide eyes on me. "It's just Zuri." I force a less strident tone. *What's wrong with me? Interaction with people my age shouldn't be this difficult.*

Zuri's admirer gives me another glance, then focuses her attention back on the needy canine. "Well, it's a cute name for a very cute puppy."

"Emerson, these are a few of my friends." Thankfully, Reid ignores my odd behavior and makes the necessary introductions. He swings an arm toward the girl swooning over Zuri. "This is Josie." With a flourish, he indicates the other two. "Ryan and Liz."

I smile at them. "It's nice to meet you."

Liz removes her hat and shakes out long, dark hair. "I can see why you'd want to spend a cold Saturday in here. This place is amazing."

Josie stands and turns toward the bookcases. Somehow during the simple move, her boot snags on the corner of the rug, causing her to trip. Almost as if he'd expected the mishap, Ryan lunges forward, catching her before she falls. The clumsy girl tosses her head back and laughs. "Liz and I always said this old lodge looked creepy and haunted. Reid, we thought your family was crazy for purchasing it. But it's beautiful."

Liz nods in agreement as she scans the room. "We grew up hearing stories about unexplained flickering lights, fluttering curtains, and slamming doors if people got too close."

"My scout leader claimed this place was once an insane asylum," Ryan adds.

A shiver courses through me.

Reid laughs off the stories. "Yeah, we heard some of those rumors when we started looking to buy the place. But nothing could change my mom's mind once she fell in love with it."

Ryan's left eyebrow arches. "Ever notice any weird paranormal activity?"

Reid shakes his head. "Nope. Nothing. Although, one of the first things we did after buying it was to have it blessed by a priest."

I expect him to show the group the hidden room, but he doesn't. For some reason, the fact that he trusted me with something not everyone knows about makes me happy.

"Do you all go to school with Reid?" I change the subject, ensuring the hidden room remains hidden.

"Yep." Ryan drapes an arm around Josie's shoulder. She leans her head against him. What a cute couple.

Reid shoves his hands into the front pockets of his jeans. "We also all attend the same church and youth group."

Liz tucks a strand of dark hair behind her ear. "And we couldn't wait to check the place out before next Saturday."

The pieces slide together in my mind. "Oh, my dad mentioned you are having a party here."

"While we liked Reid's suggestion of a skating party, we thought we'd better stop by and see what needs to be done to prepare." Liz nudges Reid. "Putting guys in charge of a party is a little risky."

He grins and elbows her back.

Their interaction makes me ponder the situation. Josie and Ryan are obviously a couple. Are Reid and Liz dating? Not wanting to intrude on their double date, I reach down to pick up the book I was reading. "Well, I'll get out of your way."

"No!" Josie throws up her hand. "Please stay and help us." Her eyes widen as she gives me a silent plea. "And you've got to come to the party."

Liz nods in agreement. "We have so much to do. We could really use your help. That is, if you're interested."

Unsure, I glance at Reid, who smiles at me and holds up a paper bag. "This is such a serious undertaking that we've brought food to help us concentrate."

Liz rolls her eyes and snatches the bag from his hand. "The guys kept arguing about which sandwich was the best, so they ordered extras in order to have a taste test and settle the issue once and for all. So, we've got plenty of food."

Before I know it, we're all sitting around one of the tables in the dining area, munching on sandwiches and chips.

Ryan points toward the porch. "We'll have to remove some of that snow so we can get down to the lake."

Reid nods. "And I have great speakers we can set up. We just need a playlist."

"I can work on that," Josie offers.

Ryan shakes his head. "Oh, no. No one except you and Liz would want to skate to a bunch of show tunes. I'll work on the music."

"Fine." Josie playfully pouts and then pops a chip in her mouth.

"I already have a list of volunteers who offered to bring food." Liz wipes her hands on a napkin.

Josie points around the dining room. "We could set the food table up along that wall and a drink station over there. There's plenty of room for tables and chairs." She taps her chin. "We'll need some tablecloths."

Since I'm now a member of this party-planning committee, I feel obligated to contribute something. "Would it be possible to string Christmas lights in this room and outside?"

Josie's eyes light up. "That would be perfect!" She offers me a huge smile. "See, we totally needed your input."

As the discussion continues, I can't help but smile. It feels good hanging out with friends and just talking about everyday things. Funny thing, though…I hadn't known until now just how much I missed it.

Chapter 6

I glance around at the congregation, composed primarily of octo-genarians. Maybe Dad and I should've accepted the Stevensons' offer to attend Mass with them down in Lake Forest. It just hadn't felt right so we decided on the closer Catholic church in Her-mann. For months, we've been trudging through the motions. I can't speak for Dad, but I haven't been fully invested in my faith for a long time. I've longed to sleep my Sunday mornings away. But even though I suspect Dad might also be experiencing a lack of faith, he is determined to keep up at least some pretense of our former lives. So here we are.

Until now, I couldn't have cared less about which church we attended. I'm only here to make Dad happy, and because Mom would've wanted us to be at church. But today, the tiny parish in Hermann, Minnesota, has me rethinking my indifference. I'm giv-ing the little elderly lady leading the music the benefit of the doubt, assuming she forgot her hearing aid this morning, and that is why her singing is so off-key. I wouldn't be surprised if any stray dogs in the area set up their own chorus of howling.

The priest has a warm smile but is not the most engaging hom-ilist as he reads his sermon from a sheet of paper. He rarely looks up and keeps pushing his glasses up the bridge of his nose. Maybe he no longer scans the congregation because he can't bear to watch the nodding heads of his dozing parishioners.

As we exit the old stone church, Dad shoots me a grin. "Well, that was one to add to our list."

I'm about to agree, but thinking about our list of the most memorable churches we've visited while on vacation reminds me of how normal our lives used to be, and it's just too painful to answer. Dad flinches like he wishes he could delete his words. He must be thinking the same thing.

At the car, he holds the passenger door open for me. Once he's settled in the driver's seat, and we're waiting for the engine to warm us up, he turns to me. "I think we should start a new Sunday tradition, at least temporarily."

"Whadaya have in mind?" Anything, no matter how lame, would be better than spending another quiet Sunday together, both of us trying to forget all the noisy, fun-filled family afternoons at Grandma's house.

"Well, I hear there's a cute bed and breakfast in town that specializes in home-cooked Sunday brunches." He looks at me with raised eyebrows.

"That sounds perfect."

He shifts into gear, and we're off. Since Hermann is merely a speck on the map, we reach our destination before the car heats up.

We ring the bell of the Victorian home and a sweet, pudgy woman wearing a frilly apron over her floral dress welcomes us. Her warm smile diminishes my perpetual chill a bit. "I'm so glad you joined us today. I met your daddy yesterday when he was picking up a pizza." She wraps me in a hug. "Now that you live here, you are family." She steps back, grasping my arms as she looks at me. "I'm Mabel. My husband, Chester, and I own this place."

When her grip loosens, I fight the urge to further increase my personal space. That would be too rude to my new family member. "Nice to meet you, Mabel. I'm Emerson."

"What a beautiful name." Mabel leads us through the antique-decorated house to a large room that holds ten tables draped in lace. Fragile-looking plates decorated with tiny, colorful flowers are already set out. Two of the tables are taken. I recognize one of the elderly couples who sat in front of us at church. As we stop at the vacant table, I wonder how they got here so quickly.

Mabel takes our coats, explaining that when her children moved away, she missed cooking Sunday brunch for them. So she decided to share her love of cooking and hospitality with others. "I suppose the only problem is that you don't get much of a menu choice. Each week, I make something different. But I always have tea, scones, and fresh fruit. You came on an exceptionally good day because the featured special is my famous stuffed French toast, served with grapefruit and a side of crispy bacon."

I settle into the floral-patterned chair, my mouth watering as I think about the upcoming meal.

Dad picks up his napkin. "That sounds amazing."

Mabel lists our tea choices and then flutters off with our jackets. I give Dad an approving smile. "I have to say, this seems to be one of your better ideas."

"I'm glad you approve because there was no telling Mabel no."

She brings a plate of scones and a delicate teapot that matches the flowered dishes. Not being tea connoisseurs, Dad and I go with her recommendation: a hibiscus and blueberry blend.

"Are you enjoying living here?" Mabel asks as she pours our tea.

"It's nice so far," I answer. "The people all seem very friendly."

"Oh, they are!" Mabel replies enthusiastically. "And I should know, I've lived here for most of my life. So many people were thrilled when the Stevensons moved to the area. Now, we are happy to welcome both of you, as well."

"Thank you." Dad gives her a broad smile.

I add two sugar cubes to my tea and stir it with a delicate spoon. "Mabel, do you know much about the history of the lodge?" Maybe a local can give me some insight.

Her eyes widen. "There are more rumors than facts about that place."

I nod. "It is rather mysterious. I'm hoping to learn more about its history."

Mabel gives me a wink. "Well, you might be surprised at what you find." Before I can ask what she means, she continues. "Don't get me wrong, the place is lovely, and I so appreciate that the Stevensons are fixing it up. But some of those stories are hard to forget."

"Like what?" Intrigue flickers through my veins.

Mabel glances around and then moves closer, clearly trying not to be overheard. "My Daddy told me that Chicago mobsters used to bring bodies up here that needed to be disposed of. They dumped them in the lake."

My eyebrows lift, almost before I know what they're up to. "Really?"

She pats my hand. "At this point, only the good Lord knows." She makes the sign of the cross. "No body has ever surfaced, so maybe it's just a rumor. Of course, knowing how the Chicago mafia worked, they would have weighed down the poor corpses."

A shiver runs down my spine. Maybe I'll rethink my desire to swim in the lake this summer.

The bell on the front door jingles. Mabel waves at her new guests and then smiles at us. "Please, excuse me. Enjoy your tea."

With Mabel out of earshot, I look at Dad. "Do you think that could be true?"

He shrugs. "I doubt it. It doesn't make sense. That's a long way to drive just to dump some bodies. Think of how many other suitable places they would have driven past to reach O'Malley Lake."

I pick up my cup, hoping he's right. If only I could find out for sure.

Dad snatches one of the warm scones. "Well, whatever happened at the lodge, I like this new assignment. I'm enjoying the work, and the Stevensons are good people."

"Yes, they are. Mrs. Stevenson is spoiling us with food. And Reid and his friends even invited me to help them set up for the party they're having on Saturday."

Dad sweeps the crumbs in front of him into a neat little pile. "Sounds like it will be a fun party. Besides getting the dining room ready, I offered to clear off the back deck as well." He smiles at me. "Hanging out with a few new friends will be nice."

"Don't get too excited. I think they just needed an extra pair of hands, but it'll be good to have something to do this week besides schoolwork." *And researching the lodge.*

Dad reaches for his teacup. "Em, thanks for keeping a positive attitude. Hopefully, someday, things will get better."

I blink back the tears that threaten to flood my eyes. We'd been enjoying a nice, normal conversation. Why did he have to go and ruin it? "Well, it's certainly not your fault that our world turned upside down."

He nods. "I'm just trying to get through one day at a time and see what God wants us to learn on this new adventure."

I take a sip of my tea—a nice way to keep from making a snarky comment. I'm not sure God cares about our circumstances. He's certainly ignored the multitude of prayers I've sent Him over the last several months. Instead of hope or comfort, all I've felt is abandonment. If God has something to teach me, He's going to have to work a little harder to get my attention because I'm tired of the silent treatment, and I'm done reaching out.

Dad's eyes brighten at something behind me. I turn to see Mabel carrying two plates loaded with mounds of food. As she sets the dishes in front of us, I close my eyes and inhale the delicious aroma. Pure bliss. How could her family ever have moved away from being pampered like this?

Stupid question. I know all too well how even the best families can be torn apart.

Chapter 7

On Monday, I hurry through my math assignment in record time, not bothering to double-check my work. I'm anxious to get to the lodge, though I'm not sure why. It's not my party, but I tossed and turned half the night, thinking of all the tiny details that needed to be taken care of to get the place looking decent by Saturday. Starting with a good cleaning. Years of neglect have left more than a little dust and grime.

I load up a bucket with all the cleaning products I can find under the sink in our cabin's kitchen. Zuri leads the way, sprinting back and forth between me and the lodge. However, with the snow piled so high on either side of the trail, her zoomies are confined to a narrow, shoveled pathway.

As we near the lodge, the side door opens. Dad is a welcome sight, as I wasn't sure how I was going to open the door without dumping my heavy load in the snow.

"Great timing." I shove the bucket of supplies toward him.

"I saw you leave the cabin from the upstairs room where I was working." He looks at the items inside the bucket. "What's all this?"

I stomp the snow from my boots. "I can't have this beautiful place making a bad impression on Reid's friends."

Ignoring the hint of a smile forming on Dad's face, I walk past him to follow Zuri down the hall. In the dining room, Dad sets the cleaning supplies on one of the tables. The view out the wall of windows and glass doors has changed. A large wooden deck is now visible, as the snow that had covered it has been removed.

"You've been busy." I lift an eyebrow at Dad.

He rolls his neck. "Not quite finished, but it's coming along. I haven't gotten to the steps or the dock yet."

I notice a shovel leaning against the wall beside the glass door. "You did all that by hand?" That must have taken forever.

"I was afraid the snowblower would damage the wood." He shrugs. "It's okay. I needed a distraction this morning."

The bright sun from the windows highlights dark circles under his eyes. He got an early morning phone call, probably his weekly update. I tense. "Everything okay?"

His jaw twitches. "Nothing new. But, hey." He gestures toward several round banquet tables that are leaning against the wall. "I found these in the basement. Figured they'd be good for the party."

Realizing he won't be revealing any more, I force a smile. "You were sweet to bring them up. I'm sure they will come in handy."

He rubs one palm against his stubbly chin. "There are a bunch of wooden folding chairs down there as well. Maybe Reid can help me lug them up sometime. Hopefully they're in working order."

"I'll let him know if I see him."

Dad glances at the supplies. "He's not coming to help you clean?"

"He doesn't know I'm here. I'm guessing he'll stop by when he gets home from school."

He nods. "Well, I'd better get back to shoveling before the temperature drops." He pulls on his hat and gloves and heads outside to continue the day's monumental task.

I remove the outer garments from Zuri and myself, then grab the bucket I brought. In need of a working sink, I push through the swinging door into the industrial kitchen. It's a large space with numerous metal shelves, counters, and stainless-steel appliances. I picture the room bustling with people scurrying about, preparing meals for the lodge's guests.

When I turn the knobs on the faucet, rust-colored liquid spurts out in a loud burst. I jump at the unexpected sound. Zuri backs away, her ears plastered to her head.

"It's okay, girl." I keep my voice soft and soothing. "Just a nasty old—very old—water line. We'll have to wait a bit and see if our efforts are successful."

Despite the setback of waiting for the water to clear, I'm soon back in the library with a bucket of warm, sudsy water in one hand and a cleaning rag in the other.

Zuri sits at my feet and watches, her head cocked to one side. I laugh. "Yeah, I'm not sure where to begin, either."

Deciding to keep everything on the shelves in their exact location, I start at the far end of the room and work shelf by shelf. I carefully lift each item, wipe down the shelf, and gently clean each book and knick-knack before returning everything to its rightful spot.

I'm on my third bucket of clean water when Reid shows up. After bending down to greet Zuri, his gaze travels the room. "This place is looking great."

I step back, surveying my progress. While I haven't gotten far, my tedious efforts have made a huge difference. The dark wood gleams, and the sad, neglected books now look regal and elegant.

"I appreciate all your help. But you really didn't have to do all this." His expression changes, and he looks like a little boy who has been caught doing something naughty. "I don't know how to ever thank you. I blurted out my great idea about the skating party before thinking it through, and then had no idea how to pull it off. I was so in over my head. You saved the day."

I laugh at his sheepish look. "I didn't do all that much. Besides, Liz and Josie wouldn't have let you fail."

"We never would have gotten the place looking this good. They're too busy with rehearsals."

"Rehearsals?" I ask as I continue working.

"They're both big into theater, always preparing for some musical or play."

I glance up from the book I'm admiring. "Is Ryan in theater, too?"

Reid laughs, clearly finding the question amusing. "No. He's our star baseball player."

"Hard to believe the snow will ever melt so he can actually play."

I can't help but notice Reid's tall, fit build. "What about you? You look like an athlete."

He grins. "Oh, yeah? Want to take a guess?"

I return the clean book to the shelf. Facing him, I cross my arms. "Let's see...you have all of your teeth, so I don't think you're a hockey player. Curling seems like a good Minnesota sport." I tap my chin. "Or maybe moose racing."

He laughs again. "Nothing that exciting. Track and field."

"A runner?"

He shakes his head. "Too exhausting. Pole vaulting."

I picture him sailing over a high bar and plopping onto a large mat. "Seriously? That sounds fun and terrifying at the same time."

"How about you?" he asks.

I plunge the cleaning rag back into the warm water. "What about me?"

"What do you like to do?"

My smile fades as I wring the water from the cloth. "Oh, nothing. I really don't do anything."

Zuri lifts her head and whines. Maybe she noticed my angst. I turn back to the shelf.

Reid breaks the moment of awkward silence. "I think Zuri's trying to say that you should take up dog training."

I glance at him. "Maybe now that we live in the frozen tundra, she and I could try dog sled racing."

He pats Zuri's head. "Only if you upgrade her to some heavy-duty booties."

A giggle escapes my lips.

Reid straightens up. "Okay, boss. Put me to work."

I look at the long row of shelves in front of me and bite back a sigh. I'm not the one that needs the help. "My dad could probably use a break from the shoveling. He also mentioned a bunch of chairs in the basement that you might want to bring up."

"Sounds good. But in an hour, we have to take a cocoa break."

His suggestion brings a smile to my face. "That's the best plan I've heard all day."

I watch as he pulls on his knit hat and gloves, steps out onto the back porch and greets Dad. They shake hands and chat a moment, and then Reid reaches for the shovel and continues the massive job of clearing the remainder of the deck. I watch him work, heaving one shovel full of snow after another over the rail. The bitter cold quickly turns his cheeks red.

Zuri looks up at me and wags her tail. I rub her silky black fur. "You're right, Zur, he is awfully nice, isn't he?"

~

True to his word, Reid returns in an hour with two mugs of cocoa. Grateful for the break, I relieve him of one of the steaming cups before easing onto the red velvet sofa, careful not to spill the drink. Reid joins me, leaving a respectable distance between us.

I blow on the hot liquid before taking a tentative sip. "Mmm...this is perfect. Thanks."

Reid tilts his head and looks at me. "I wish I could take the credit, but it was all my mom's doing." He looks over the dust-free shelves. "I can't believe what a difference a little cleaning makes."

I also admire the now-gleaming shelves. The books and assorted items on the left of the fireplace show their true colors now that their gray coats have been removed. "It does look better, but if I'd known how long it would take to clean, I might have chosen another task."

His brown eyes narrow as he peers at the shelves. "Does something feel off about them?"

I lower my mug. "Yes! That's exactly what I've been thinking. I just can't figure out what's wrong."

His forehead creases. "Did you put everything back where it was?"

"I made sure not to rearrange anything." My gaze shifts between the shelves on either side of the stone fireplace. A pattern seems to emerge. "I think I know what it is. The shelves on either side of the fireplace are identical. Almost."

We both stare at the shelves, pondering my discovery. The books are arranged the same way, as are the knick-knacks. Stone busts of grumpy, old men reside on the third shelf of both bookcases. Carved book ends surround eight books in the center of the fourth shelf. Wooden ducks face away from the fireplaces on the top shelves. The two bookcases are mirror images of each other—except for the second shelf. The bookcase on the left holds a framed picture of the lodge, and a decorative box sits next to a pile of books, their decreasing size giving the pile a slight pyramid structure. A pinecone supplies the pinnacle to the shape. In contrast, the bookcase on the right holds only the pinecone, which lies on its side, alone and abandoned, with no books to rest on.

"Guess someone never returned the stack of books." I sip my cocoa, happy to have finally figured out what has bothered me about this room.

"Good eye. As we clean up this place, we'll have to keep an eye out for the missing books."

His phones buzzes, and he glances at it. "I've got to go pick up Raina."

When he stands, I reach for his mug. "My turn to supply the treat tomorrow."

He grins and hands over the empty cup. "Deal." Grabbing his jacket from the back of the sofa, he clears his throat. "You staying awhile?"

I shake my head. "Nah, I think I've done enough for one day. Probably better go start dinner."

He holds out a hand to help me up. I hesitate momentarily, then shift both mugs to one hand and place my free hand in his. His touch sends a surprising spark of heat from my head to my toes.

Once we are both bundled for the cold, we leave the lodge. The mugs and thermos now reside in the bucket that swings from my hand, and Zuri calmly walks between us.

Reid trails his gloved hand along the wall of snow we're passing. When he looks my way, a mischievous grin plays on his lips. Before I know it, he flicks some of the icy crystals in my direction. Shocked by the cold, I open my mouth to protest.

He laughs and wipes the snow from my face. "Sorry. I couldn't resist."

I shove him in a playful push, which excites Zuri, who's always ready to play. She leaps up, her front paws also landing on his chest.

Reid laughs. "Hey, two on one—not fair!" He jumps sideways. Eager to rough house, Zuri bounds toward him again. The two of them begin a lively game of sprint-and-spin, zig and zag.

I laugh at their antics. "Don't you know never to mess with a girl and her dog?"

Playfully trying to escape Zuri, Reid steps behind me and grabs my arms, using me as a human shield. This excites Zuri even more, and she runs in circles.

The silliness makes me realize that poor Zuri has probably been missing our old life as well. I pledge to be a better pet owner. She deserves more than my prolonged depression. We both do.

Chapter 8

Thanks to a long online Q&A session, my schoolwork takes longer than expected. By the time I close my laptop, both Zuri and I are stir-crazy. We've been holed up in the cabin long enough.

I bundle us up, but instead of heading straight to the lodge, we locate a path that takes us closer to the lake. Although I'm awkward in my boots, I manage to jog along the way. The activity serves two purposes. My movement amps up Zuri's excitement as she sprints around me. So she gets a little more exercise, and I keep slightly warmer.

The sun is starting to break through the clouds that have hovered over the area all morning, making the scene that unfolds before us breathtaking. In the shifting light, the icy lake and old lodge appear mysterious and picturesque at the same time, like something from a movie. I'm still unsure of the genre—romance or horror. I make a silent vow to carve out more time to research the place and satisfy my curiosity.

From this angle, Dad and Reid's progress in clearing the large deck of its snow coat is apparent. The glass doors from the dining hall open to an expansive deck, a wide staircase and a path that leads down to a white gazebo and a dock. Both look inviting, despite their peeling paint.

As much as I love the view, the inactivity of admiring the improvements chills me, so Zuri and I head toward the lodge.

Today, a country song lures me down the hallway to the lobby, where Dad and Mr. Stevenson work in companionable silence. The twangy tune plays from a small speaker resting on the check-in counter. Dad towers overhead from atop a tall ladder as he works on the antler chandelier. Mr. Stevenson, almost in direct opposition, greases the hinges of the massive front door from a kneeling position.

Zuri greets the men with a friendly bark.

Dad peers down at me. "Hey, kid. How was class?"

"Definitely a middle-class kind of day." I beat him to the punchline of a lame dad joke that he seems to think is funny but has never made sense to me.

He and Mr. Stevenson chuckle in unison.

"You here to finish cleaning the bookshelves?" Dad asks.

"Yep." I sit on the bottom step of the grand staircase with Zuri to begin the tedious process of removing our protective gear. When I pull off my knit hat, my hair spazzes in staticky frizz. I attempt to smooth out the flyaways and resecure my ponytail.

Mr. Stevenson stands and tilts his head to one side and then the other to work out a kink in his neck. "Thank you, Emerson. You've done an amazing job on the bookshelves. I know Reid appreciates your help."

"It's been oddly fun." Wow. Has cleaning really become the highlight of my days? Pathetic.

I bid them farewell and head for the kitchen to fill my bucket of soapy water, then I'm back in the library. After setting the heavy pail on the floor, I peer at the shelves, focusing on the one that lacks its stack of books. Now that I've determined what bothered me about the two bookcases, my gaze goes straight to the empty spot. Then it hits me—a crystal-clear vision of the missing stack of books. Of course! I had seen them…in the secret room.

Setting down the bucket, I walk toward the bookcase on the far wall, hoping I remember how Reid opened the hidden door. Fortunately, it swings open. Good thing I paid close attention. With Zuri on my heels, we enter the dim room. Since I won't be long, I don't bother searching for the light switch. Although, being in the shadowy room without Reid does make my nerves percolate.

Still, it's gratifying to see I was not mistaken. The stack of books is right there on the high-top table, just as I remembered. I move closer to get a better look. Which classics will be in this stack? The titles are hard to read in the dim light, so I gather up the pile, eager to put the books back where they belong, and balance out the weirdly off-kilter library shelf.

I nearly trip over Zuri when she pounces in front of me and goes a bit wild, scratching at the floor. My heart races. She'd better not have found a mouse. I study her movements, eyes narrowed. If she's in hunter-mode, I'll probably need to pull her away from some disease-carrying rodent. But the saucy tail wag and floor-pawing seem to indicate otherwise. On closer inspection, I see it's a mere beam of light that has captured her attention. What a goof.

"Come on, silly girl. Let's get to work."

I take two steps toward the doorway, then stop. Turning back, I stare at the sliver of brightness that has captured my dog's attention. How can natural light shine in a room without windows? I scan the walls, making sure I didn't miss a boarded-up pane, but there are none. Setting the books back on the table, I bend over, searching for the source of the light.

And there it is. I spot a thin crack in the wall behind the table, about six inches above the floorboards. Another hidden room? Curiosity takes charge, dispelling all apprehension. I shove the table aside, then feel along the wall, searching for a button or a latch of some sort, like the one used to enter this space. Zuri patiently watches me work. I slide my hand runs along the rough wood panels until I come to a spot where the texture changes. It's completely smooth. I place both hands on the spot and push. Nothing. Undeterred, I apply more force until the wall finally gives under the pressure, shifting backward a few inches with a groan of protest. I wiggle my fingers into the opening and, with a final push, slide the panel to the right.

Zuri lets out a low whine. I pat my thigh, and she joins me. Together, we peer inside the new space—a long, windowless hallway. But high on the wall I spot what looks like an air duct. That's where the light is coming from. I marvel at the thin slots. Only the perfect angle of the sun shining through the slats would hit the crack in the wall, making the beam visible in the adjoining room.

I shine the light on my phone down the mysterious hallway. Cobwebs make for a less-than-inviting space. The creepiness from finding yet another hidden piece of the house, amid all of the disturbing rumors surrounding this place, keeps me from exploring on my own.

Backing out, I leave the hallway just as I found it.

~

Reid arrives as I finish cleaning the final bookcase.

"Hey, it looks amazing!"

"Oh, no! You're here already."

He grins as Zuri wriggles up against his leg. "Well, at least one of you is happy to see me."

I blow an errant tendril of blonde hair out of my line of sight, not wanting to use my hands and risk smearing grime across my face. "I lost track of time and forgot to get the ingredients for the cocoa I promised."

He holds a hand to his heart. "My day is ruined."

"Well, don't fret." I drop my rag in the bucket and wipe my hands on my leggings. "I have something even better to show you."

He unzips his jacket. "You made chocolate chip cookies?"

I readjust my ponytail, gathering all the strands that escaped as I worked. "Well, maybe it's not *that* good. But I think you'll be intrigued."

Reid follows me to the far wall. I open the hidden door, and we enter the billiards room. He points to the table where I'd found the books. "Wow. I *am* impressed. You cleared the dust in a perfect rectangle."

Giving him a sarcastic eyeroll, I proceed to move the table. Soon, I'm opening the newly discovered door. Turning to him, I spread my arms wide. "Ta-da!"

His mouth hangs open. "Whoa." Walking closer, he peers into the shadowy space. "How'd you find this?"

While I explain, Reid pulls out his phone and shines a light into the narrow space.

He steps back and looks at me, his brow creased. "Have you shown our dads yet?"

I shake my head. "Not yet. I wanted you to be the first, well, *second* to know." Zuri whines her objection. "Okay, make that the third to know."

He smiles, then arches on eyebrow. "Want to explore?"

"I thought you'd never ask."

He takes a tentative step into the dark space. I follow along, and with an excited yip, Zuri joins us. We're forced to travel single file in the dusty hallway. Within a few steps, our caution becomes too much for the canine member of our exploration team. She maneuvers around our legs to lead the way.

Despite the light from Reid's phone, it's hard to keep an eye on my black dog in the dark, windowless space. A few light beams sneak through the old siding, but vision is limited at best. I pull out my phone and add my light to Reid's, then scan the walls for any sign of another hidden compartment. In the semi-darkness—and yes, not watching where I'm going—I slam into Reid, my nose smashing against his shoulder.

"Oh! Sorry." I rub my nose and try to peer around him. "Find something?"

"You could say that." He flattens himself against the wall so I can have a better view.

The beam from my phone reveals a wooden staircase curving up into darkness. Zuri sits near the bottom step, looking very proud of her discovery. I scratch her head, then turn to Reid. The small beam of light shadows his features, making it difficult to see his expression, but I'm pretty sure his brow is furrowed once again.

"Shall we see where this leads?" he asks.

I gesture for him to continue. "I'm game if you are."

He slowly moves up the stairs, testing each step before putting his whole weight on it. Not wanting to put extra strain on the old structure, I wait at the bottom, shining my light up to offer some help, but I'm pretty sure the little beam is useless.

His footsteps stop. "I reached the top. Let me see if this door opens." The old wood groans as if it's unhappy to be disturbed after so many years. Soon, he disappears from sight.

My growing curiosity finally overtakes my patience. "What do you see?"

My query is met with silence.

"Reid?" Nothing. He'd better not be messing with me.

I strain to hear even the softest sound. The faint creak of footsteps reaches my ears.

"Come on up." His voice is slightly muffled, like he's standing quite a distance from me.

I tighten my grip on the railing and ascend the stairs. Zuri's toenails click on the steps as she follows close behind. At the top of the dark staircase, my beam partially illuminates Reid where he waits for me. The shadows provide a ghoulish vibe, creeping me out.

He reaches out a hand. "Careful."

I tentatively take his hand and enter a musty-smelling room. My phone's light reveals a closet-sized space. The only item in the room is a dresser against one wall. My shoulders droop with disappointment at the dead end.

I'm ready to leave, but Reid sets his phone on top of the dresser, the light shining toward the ceiling.

"It doesn't make sense for this to lead nowhere," he says. "I bet this room connects to one of the guest rooms. Maybe the entrance is covered. Help me push this out of the way."

I pocket my phone and join him in moving the dresser. At first, it doesn't budge, but then the heavy piece of furniture gives up its resistance, creaking as we dislodge it from a position held for who knows how long. I retrieve my phone and shine it on the wall.

We share a smile, then look back at the square opening about a foot off the floor. Crouching down, we peer through the hole in the wall and find a small passageway about two feet tall and two feet long. A sliver of light cuts horizontally through the center of the space.

Reid reaches through the opening and pushes on the back of the mysterious passageway. Cupboard doors fling open, letting in afternoon light.

Once Reid indicates I should go first, I maneuver through the small space and find myself in one of the lodge's guest rooms. A metal four-poster bed with a saggy mattress takes up most of the space. Drab, flowery curtains hang from windows that line the wall on the right. This must be the last room on this side of the building. Beside the bed is an upholstered chair. I picture dust billowing up to choke me if I sit in it, which I have no intention of doing.

I turn to see what I crawled through and realize it's an armoire, just like in *The Lion, the Witch, and the Wardrobe*. So cool. El absolutely loves that book. I'll have to tell her…I catch myself before my mind finishes the thought.

Zuri leaps through the cupboard in one fluid movement and begins sniffing the floorboards. A minute later, Reid manages to squeeze his long frame through the little tunnel.

Standing, he surveys the room, then looks at me with a grin. "Well, that's certainly unexpected."

I stare at him in amazement. "I wonder what other secrets this place has to offer."

His eyes light up and his smile widens. "The plot thickens."

I nod and force myself not to bite the inside of my lip—a bad habit I'm trying to break. "I guess we'll just have to keep exploring."

And spending more time together.

~

Dad chews a bite of his dinner and takes a sip of water. Finally, he looks up and notices I'm staring at him. He frowns in obvious confusion.

I let out a huff of frustration. "You aren't at all intrigued by the new hidden passageway?"

He sets down his fork. "Don't get me wrong. I *do* find it fascinating. But another hidden room doesn't seem that surprising."

"Well, I'm curious enough for the both of us. I'm thinking of going to the library in town tomorrow to see if I can uncover anything interesting about the people who built this place. Can I take your truck?"

Dad studies me for a moment, then swallows another drink of water before answering. "Can you assure me you'll limit your online searches?"

I look down at my plate, trying to hide my percolating emotions. "You don't think I learned that lesson?"

He reaches out and places a calloused hand on mine. "Em, I'm sorry. I'm happy that you're taking an interest in something. But I'm your father, and it's my job to worry."

I look up and hold his gaze for a few beats, waiting out the internal battle of how to respond. Avoiding an Emotional Scene is crowned the victor. My hand slides out from under his, and I raise it to give my oath.

"I solemnly swear to limit my research to the history of the lodge and its previous occupants."

He smirks as his hand retreats to his side of the table.

"Hey, speaking of the lodge," I say, "do you think the dining room will be ready for the party on Saturday?" A pretty smooth transition, if I do say so myself.

"Yes, I've completed my part." He reaches for another slice of garlic bread, then uses it to point at me. "Now, you and your friends need to make it look good."

"Dad, they're not my friends. I met them once."

"But you'll get to know them better at the party." He chomps into the crispy bread.

While he's trying to be subtle, I see right through him. Not only is he hoping I'll start hanging out with Reid and his friends, but also that I'll want to start attending their youth group and re-discover my faith. But honestly, I don't know how I feel about faith in general right now. I took everyone's advice and prayed a lot while our world was dealt such a seismic blow, but everyone telling me to pray felt cliché, just the thing to say when trouble struck. None of my prayers were answered anyway, so I'm taking a bit of a break.

I shrug. "I don't know if I'll go. It's been fun getting to know Reid's friends, but meeting a bunch of new people sounds tiring."

His eyes soften as he looks at me. "I know. But we can't live our lives in isolation."

I grin. "This from the man who literally moved us to one of the most isolated places on the planet."

He laughs. "Touché."

My fork swirls through the remains of my dinner. "Dad, do you ever think about them?"

"Every moment of every day." He reaches out and rests his hand on mine again. This time I find the warmth soothing. "Em, what happened was not your fault. And, most importantly, we're going to get through it."

I sure hope he's right, but I don't see how.

Chapter 9

The moment I close my laptop the following day, Zuri stands and stretches. A noisy yawn, more fitting of an old man than a dog, escapes her gaping jaws.

"Sorry, but I can't take you with me today."

Her ears lift as she cocks her head to the side.

"But I'll let you out before I leave."

Her tail wags in excitement.

I'd finished my schoolwork quickly, despite having trouble with concentration. Hopefully, my grades won't suffer too much due to all the distractions that have captivated my attention lately.

Unsatisfied after her quick walk, Zuri whines her displeasure as I shut the door between us, leaving her behind. I trudge to the truck and start the engine. My internal temperature cools one degree at a time as the vehicle slowly warms up. When they finally reach a happy equilibrium, I point the truck toward town. The grating noise of the tires crunching across the crisp snow sends a shiver down my spine.

The sun has stubbornly refused to make an appearance today. Its absence cloaks the area in a depressing shade of gray. Anxious to delve into some research, I ignore the atmospheric gloominess. No telling what fascinating information I'm about to uncover. I'm tempted to press harder on the accelerator, but I want to make it to the library in one piece.

Twenty minutes later, I pull into an empty parking space in front of the all-encompassing library/coffee shop/hall of records, eager to start my investigation.

I push open the thick glass door, triggering a bell that alerts everyone inside to look up and straight at me. The teenaged barista in the coffee area to my left also sends a bored glance my way before her gaze returns to her phone. I approach the counter in front of me, drawn by the large "INFORMATION" sign hanging above it. A middle-aged woman with curly red hair stands and offers a welcoming smile.

"Good afternoon. May I help you?"

"Yes, please. I'm hoping to research the history of the lodge at O'Malley Lake. Do you have any records I could look at?"

Her penciled-in eyebrows raise. She eyes me closer. "You must be the Stevensons' contractor's daughter."

"Guilty as charged."

She laughs. "Sorry. No offense. We don't get many new folks in town, so word travels fast." Her Minnesota accent, overpronouncing the long *o*'s, makes me smile. "Are you enjoying the area?"

"Yes, the lake is beautiful, and I've become rather intrigued by the lodge."

Her red curls bounce as she nods. "Join the club. I'm Mrs. Grier, by the way." She sticks out her hand, revealing nail polish the same shade as her hair.

I accept the handshake. "Nice to meet you. I'm Emerson."

"What a pretty name."

"Thanks. I've always liked it. So, do you know much about the lodge?"

"Mostly just rumors."

"I heard there was a mysterious death there," I dig a little, determined not to be stymied in my investigation as easily as that. Rumors are most often based on at least a shred of truth.

She glances at the bored barista, and then back at me. "I've heard on good authority that when Mr. O'Malley returned from World War II, he wasn't quite right. Of course, who wouldn't be affected by that horrible war? But he had more trouble than most in coping with life afterward. He became a recluse. And then his wife suddenly died." Her voice lowers in a conspiratorial tone.

"Since she was fairly young and in good health, it was quite unexpected."

"Do you know her cause of death?" I query.

She leans closer to me. "Apparently, there wasn't much of an investigation. And, it turns out, the sheriff at the time was Mr. O'Malley's cousin, which added fuel to the rumors of foul play."

Armed with that bit of information, I follow her to the archive room. Before long, books, digitized historical records, and binders of old newspapers cover the table in front of me.

I delve into my research, jotting down the basics I uncover.

State census data shows that James O'Malley left Tipperary, Ireland, at the beginning of the potato famine. In 1851, soon after the Minnesota Territory was established, the government provided incentives for settlers and O'Malley homesteaded the land at the lake.

A newspaper article reveals that the speculative bubble burst in 1857, when the banks back east called in their loans. But James O'Malley somehow persevered.

After scouring some old county documents, I discover it was James O'Malley III who had the lodge built in 1912.

Turning to the archived newspapers, I find an article about the many Chicagoans who traveled to various Minnesota lakes each summer to escape the city's stifling heat.

Finally, a human-interest story shows up about James O'Malley V and his return from World War II. The accompanying photo of a young, wide-eyed soldier who looks completely overwhelmed makes me remember Mrs. Grier saying James wasn't the same when he returned home.

"Hey!"

Startled, I whip a glance upward and bite down on a lip that wants to smile.

Reid leans against the doorjamb, his gaze fixed on me. "Whatcha doing here?"

I catch my breath on a small burst of excitement. "Hi! How'd you know I'd be here?"

He scans the documents laid out before me. "I didn't. I was picking up a library book for my mom. Doing research for a class?"

"No." I stretch my back, suddenly aware that it is none-too-pleased about being hunched over the table for way too long. "I'm trying to discover more about the lodge."

His eyebrows raise in surprise, then he sits across the table from me. "So what've you found out?"

I spend the next few minutes telling him about the O'Malleys.

"No mention of what the hidden tunnel and room were for?"

I shake my head. "Nope. I'm not giving up but further research will have to wait until after the party."

He holds up a piece of paper. "Speaking of the party, Mom sent me out with a long list of things to buy. If you feel like taking a break from your research, I could use some help with the shopping." He looks at the paper. "What the heck are tea lights, and where should a guy look for them?"

His pathetic expression makes me laugh. "I do believe my assistance might cut down on the hours you would otherwise spend roaming around the grocery store."

Reid helps me gather my research items, then crosses his arms and taps his foot against the tile floor with feigned impatience as I bundle up in layer upon layer of outer gear. When I'm finally ready to face the elements, we leave the room.

I wave a mittened hand at Mrs. Grier. "Thanks so much for helping me."

She jumps from her seat to hand me a folder. "I found this as well. It won't give you any facts, as it deals more with the rumors that swirl about the place. But it might be fun to read."

I share an excited glance with Reid, and then reach for the folder she's offering me. "Thank you so much." I slide it into my bag, next to my notebook. Maybe the new information will shed some light on the mysterious rooms.

Once outside, I make a beeline to the truck.

"Where are you going?" Reid asks.

I turn to look at him as a wind gust swirls around us. "I'm parked right here. I can drive us."

He points down the block. "We don't need to drive. The store's just a block away."

"Reid, it's freezing out here."

He grins. "Then we better get moving."

My huff is accentuated by a cloud of billowy, hot air. "At least let me drop off my bag." I unlock the truck and toss my backpack inside without waiting for his permission. After closing the door, I join him on the sidewalk.

Reid leads the way, while I do my best turtle impression and sink further down inside my thick scarf. Just about the time I'm unable to feel my toes, we arrive at the store. My gallant escort pulls open the door, and I gratefully enter the heated building.

As I uncoil my scarf, I glance around, acquainting myself with the place. The general store isn't huge, but from the signs above each aisle, it's clear that it carries just about any of the basics one might need—groceries, home goods, clothing, hardware, and even livestock items.

I hold out my hand. "Okay, let's see that list of yours."

Reid surrenders the neatly hand-printed list. I scan the items while he dislodges a shopping cart from its friends and wheels it over. Although I could spend a great deal of time at a mall, I've never cared much for grocery shopping. Still, exploring the aisles with Reid becomes a surprisingly entertaining way to spend a bitterly cold afternoon. Our squeaky-wheeled cart begins to fill up with decorations and food for the party.

Checking items off our list as we go, we pass from the food aisles to the clothing section. In the outerwear department, Reid stops the cart in front of a large clearance bin. He rifles through the items, finally pulling out a festive elf hat. He presents it to me with a deep bow. "For you, milady. Maybe not completely stylish, but it looks warm."

"Sir Knight, you're most thoughtful." I reach for fuzzy, pink earmuffs, partially hidden beneath a leopard-print scarf, and toss them to him with a grin. "I wouldn't want to be the only one enjoying new gear."

He plops them on his head. "How do they look?"

Adorable is the first word that comes to mind, but I quickly choose a different descriptor. "Incredible." I pull the elf hat over my blonde hair and slowly turn in a circle, modeling the new attire. "Does it go with my outfit?"

"Definitely." His eyes widen, a look of mischief sliding onto his face. "But don't take my word for it."

Reid pulls me toward one of those little photo booths. I laugh and slide into the tiny space. He squishes in next to me and yanks the curtain closed. Fishing a dollar from his wallet, he inserts it into the machine. When prompted, we strike three silly poses as the camera flashes. Two identical strips of three photos soon emerge from the machine. He hands me one.

We look ridiculous— of course—but I'm suddenly aware that it's the first photo I've been in since before everything happened. The happy expression on my face in the three goofy shots fills me with irrational guilt. The strip quivers in my trembling hand—for once, the shaking is not from the cold.

I've stared at the photo for far too long. I glance up to find Reid watching me, his playful smile replaced with a somber expression I can't quite decipher. He probably thinks I'm a complete psycho.

I wave the photo strip between us. "I'm just not sure the emerald green of this hat goes with my complexion. But you, sir…" I shake my head in make-believe seriousness. "You really rock those pink earmuffs. I suggest you wear them to your party."

His grin returns, and he slides out of the booth. "Well, if you're not feeling the elf hat, we'll have to find you something else because I don't think you have anything adequate for nighttime ice skating."

I stand and pull the hat off my head. Then I glance in a nearby mirror to tamp down any staticky strands. "Oh, don't worry about that, I won't be attending."

Behind my own reflection in the mirror, Reid's puzzlement creases his forehead. "Why not? You have something more exciting scheduled?"

I turn to face him. "No. But I'm not going to crash your party."

"You can't crash something you've been invited to. I'd really like you to go. You've already met Josie, Ryan, and Liz. The others are all pretty low-key as well." His hands press together in a prayer position. "Come on, it'll be fun."

"Did my dad put you up to this?" I need to know the motivation behind his insistence.

"Put me up to what?" His confusion seems genuine.

"Inviting me. It seems like something he would do."

Reid shakes his head and his hands open in surrender. "Honestly, he hasn't said any such thing."

The shake of his head puts an end to the topic because trying to continue our serious conversation while he's still sporting the pink earmuffs is no longer possible.

A giggle bubbles forth. "I wish Raina could see you now."

He chuckles and pulls off the silly headgear. "I'd never live it down."

I fan myself with the photo strip. "Well, I have proof. And I'm not afraid to use it."

He looks offended. "Emerson! I never took you for the kind of person who would resort to blackmail."

I shrug. "You don't know me well enough to make that determination."

"Fair enough. Okay, what are your demands?"

I start walking back to our abandoned cart. "Unknown for now. But I'm going to hang onto the opportunity, because I'm sure it will come in handy at some point." I drop the elf hat back in the clearance bin.

Reid tosses the earmuffs on top of the pointed-eared abomination, and then holds up his photo strip. "Well, don't forget that I also have evidence of our malfeasance, and I'm not afraid to use it, either."

My eyes narrow. "Really? And what leverage do you possess?"

He shoots me a wicked grin. "I'll show Zuri that you were having fun without her."

I gasp in mock distress, then insert a note of disdain in my voice. "You play dirty. Fine. What do you want?"

His eyes sparkle. "You have to attend the party."

I cave. Again. I should be stronger, but one can resist a handsome boy for only so long. And Reid is far beyond simply handsome. "Okay, fine, I'll go."

"Great!" He turns to the shelves of winter gear. "But I was serious. We need to get you some warmer items. You will not develop hypothermia on my watch."

A flood of warmth washes over me as he roots through the outerwear selection. I'm still not convinced Dad didn't have something to do with the invitation, but it doesn't matter. Despite my protests, having something to look forward to feels pretty amazing.

Chapter 10

I do my best to stay focused on my school assignments the following morning, but my mind keeps drifting to all that I'd learned about the O'Malley family. The reading material Mrs. Grier sent home kept me up way too late.

She'd uncovered a local magazine article from the 1970s that covered the various rumors about the lodge. Apparently, after James O'Malley V returned from the war, he hired several contractors to update the place. Each company worked on different parts of the property, fueling speculation that he was up to something suspicious. Stories quickly spread about numerous odd events at the lodge, so when it re-opened, few people wanted to stay there.

The article mentioned some of the mysterious stories about the lodge being haunted. Others thought the Chicago guests brought organized crime to the area. After his wife's unexpected death, James became even more of a recluse, and the lodge closed. Eventually, he was found dead in the woods by local hunters. Decay had made it difficult to determine the cause of death.

The most intriguing part of the article was about Caroline, a maid who had worked at the lodge. She claimed to have discovered a secret door in one of the guest rooms. She gave a detailed description of being in one of the rooms and making the bed while the morning sun shone through the window, lighting up the floorboards. She noticed scratch marks on the floor and bent to see if polishing the boards would make the marks less noticeable. The gouges lined up with the dresser, like it had been pushed away from the wall. After further exploration, she discovered a movable section in the wall behind the dresser. I fell asleep, feeling an odd connection with this woman who'd also found the secret passageway.

Bleary-eyed from my restless night, I struggle to concentrate on my online quiz as the morning sun shines through the kitchen window, blinding me with its brightness. Caroline's account rolls around in my head and nags at my thoughts, distracting me further. The maid specifically commented on the morning sun. If her memory was correct, she hadn't been describing the room Reid and I had discovered because when we entered the upstairs guest room, the afternoon sun was coming in through the windows. The room Caroline described must be on the opposite end of the lodge.

The corner rooms right above the side entrance I always use would be most affected by the morning sun, so that's where I'll be exploring this afternoon.

Once my homework is completed, Zuri and I make the short journey to the lodge. While we walk, I compose a letter to Keira in my head. I'd weaned myself from the habit since we'd moved here, but today, I can't help myself.

Oh, Kiera, how I wish you were here. You'd love this place. Dad has been tasked with fixing up this old lodge. At first, I had no interest in our new home, but this place hides some incredible secrets, and I'm determined to figure them out. However, I've never gone off on my own for an adventure. I sure could use my BFF right about now. But Zuri is helping me, as well as this cute guy named Reid. I know, I know, I promise I won't get too attached. But it's nice to have someone to hang out with again. Miss you always. ~ Em

We enter the side door, and I take my time strolling down the hallway to the main entrance. Zuri has no patience for my melancholy and zooms ahead, sprinting up the staircase. I follow, more slowly, while she scurries into each room, briefly checking them out. Finished with her thorough search, she joins me in the room at the end of the hallway that faces away from the lake, overlooking the circular drive and front porch. Windows evenly line the two outer walls. The third wall runs parallel to the hallway. The room's bathroom is on the other side of the final wall. I scan the walls, but after quickly concluding that there are no hidden rooms, I move across the hall.

Here, red and gold wallpaper covers the top half of the walls. Above the chair rail, the decorative print is peeling away, but otherwise it appears to be in good condition—aside from being terribly outdated. Below the wood trim of the chair rail are decorative panels of dark wood. My gaze narrows in to scrutinize the four walls of the room in search of another hidden door. The wall adjacent to the hallway seems normal, as does the wall with the bathroom doorway. That leaves the two window walls. Nothing seems out of place with the windows situated at the end of the lodge. Below is the driveway with the shoveled walkway that veers off to the right and our little cabin. Reid's house sits directly in front of me, about fifty yards further down the driveway.

I turn to the wall facing the lake. The bay window offers an inviting window seat and a spectacular view of the ice-covered body of water. I hadn't noticed before, but while the window bows out two feet from the wall, it doesn't seem to protrude at all from the lodge. On the left side of the window is a door which leads to a small closet. To the right is a plain section of wall. Interesting. There must be two feet of wasted space behind this wall that would fit a dresser quite nicely. I look at the floor, and sure enough, the floorboards bear scratch marks. Bending down, I examine the wall, and find a panel insert that isn't flush against the wood chair rail. I push on it gently, and it gives way, popping back to reveal a square opening.

Zuri scurries over and tilts her head to the side. I scratch behind her ear. "I'm curious, too. Should we explore?"

She lets out a sharp, excited bark.

"All right, then. Let's do this."

I tap the flashlight app on my phone and crawl through the hole, hoping no spiderwebs attach to my hair. Behind me, Zuri's nails click and clack as she follows along. I emerge into a tight, closet-like space. My light shines on another spiral staircase, tucked into the corner of the lodge, just like the one Reid and I found on the opposite side of the building.

I look down at Zuri, who I can barely make out in the darkness. "Think we should wait for Reid?"

She tilts her head to the side.

"It's not that I'm scared. I just think he'd enjoy checking it out, too."

Her tail thumps in agreement, sending up a cloud of dust.

Stifling a cough, I turn to reenter the bedroom and notice a metal box attached to the wall. My grandparents used to have a mailbox that looked exactly like this. I lift the lid and peer inside, pulling in a sharp breath when I spot a folded piece of paper. A letter? A note for someone in the room? I pocket whatever it is before exiting the creepy space. I'll wait for Reid and we can look at it together.

Luckily for my curiosity, I don't have long to wait. Through the bedroom window, I see him stomping through the snow toward the lodge. I take a step away from the window, not wanting him to see me watching him, but my ploy is ruined by my dog. When Zuri spies Reid, she charges the window. With her paws on the sill, she unleashes a barking frenzy, her whole body wiggling along with her tail. The old windowpanes are hardly soundproof, so despite the knit hat covering his ears, Reid clearly hears the ruckus and looks up. I know from experience that my black dog is hard to see through the reflection of windows, so I step forward and wave. Reid already knows we're watching from somewhere, anyway. He smiles and waves back.

I turn and glare at Zuri. "Sometimes it's better to be more discreet."

Her ears perk as I playfully scold. Then, completely ignoring my suggestion, she dashes out of the room to search for Reid. Sighing, I tag along.

By the time I reach the top of the steps, Reid and Zuri are trotting up toward me. Zuri has a white rawhide bone clenched between her teeth.

"Aww, thanks for bringing her a treat."

He shrugs. "I felt bad that we had a whole excursion yesterday without her."

I stare at him for a moment, touched by his incredibly sweet gesture.

His cheeks slightly redden. "Okay. I guess that sounds pretty lame."

I smile. "No. I understand. She is a master manipulator."

"I couldn't face her disappointed puppy dog eyes, so I came prepared." He shoves his hands into his front pockets. "So, what have you two been up to?"

Excitement zips through my veins. "Want to see?"

His head tilts. "Did you find something?"

I can't control my smile. We walk down the hall to the last room while I tell him about my research. When we reach our destination, his gaze darts to the open hole in the wall.

"You found another hidden door. Where does this one lead?"

I shrug. "I don't know. I waited for you before exploring."

His smile crinkles the skin around his eyes.

My cheeks begin to warm under his gaze. I pull the note I found in the mailbox from my sweatshirt pocket. "I found this as well."

His gaze shifts from the note to my face. "What does it say?"

Despite my best attempt to control my reaction, I'm sure my blush is deepening. "I didn't want to read it without you." I hold it out toward him.

"Well, let's find out." He steps closer, and suddenly, I'm feeling a little woozy from the intensity of his chocolate-brown eyes and his scent—a mixture of mint, spruce, and confidence.

Trying to control the slight tremor in my hand, I unfold the yellowed paper. He reaches out, steadying the paper with one hand.

Meet me at the drop point tomorrow night for the next delivery.

I reread the cryptic message. What were the O'Malleys up to? Is this an innocent request about a standard delivery, or something more sinister? Disappointment sinks in. So much for a grand clue—this is essentially useless. I turn to catch Reid's reaction, but instead of looking at the paper, his eyes shift to something over my shoulder.

"We've got company." He frowns as he releases his hold on the note.

I follow his gaze out the window to see three figures walking toward the lodge. Their arms are loaded with bags. Bundled in scarves and hats, I'm unable to see the faces of the trio, but from their sizes and choice of winter coats, it appears to be two females and one guy.

"Is that Josie, Ryan, and Liz?" I ask. "I didn't realize they were coming today."

Reid shakes his head. "Me, neither." A tinge of annoyance colors his answer, which makes me smile. I'm not the only one who thinks his friends have lousy timing.

We watch as one of the girls attempts a twirl but slips. In an oddly smooth movement, she falls sideways into the tall snowbank. The right side of her body disappears into the white wall. Impressively, she doesn't drop either of the bags she's holding. Ryan shakes his head, and then sets down his bags to extricate her from her predicament.

Reid and I both cringe.

"Was that Josie?" I ask.

He lets out a chuckle. "Without a doubt. She's a bit of a walking hazard."

I hold up the yellowed paper. "Guess our mystery will have to wait."

A shadow passes across his face that I like to believe is regret. "Guess so."

I return the note to my pocket, and we leave the room to greet the others.

By the time we reach the lobby, Reid's friends are stomping the snow from their boots, peeling away layers of clothing, and greeting Zuri.

Josie's face is bright red from her unfortunate meeting with the snowbank, but her eyes light up when she sees us. "Hey, there! Reid, your mom said you would be here."

"I'm surprised to see you," Reid responds. "I thought you had rehearsal all week."

"The heater in the theater wasn't working, so rehearsal was canceled," Liz explains.

"That's awesome." Reid's tone doesn't quite match his words.

Liz must notice Reid's less-than-enthusiastic response. She looks from Reid to me, then back to Reid. "Oh, sorry. We should have given you a heads-up."

Before the others can assume they interrupted something more scandalous than solving a mystery, I reach for one of the bags Liz is holding. "Don't be silly. This is great. I was afraid we wouldn't have enough time on Saturday to get this place decorated."

Josie loops her arm around mine and leads the way into the dining room, leaving the items she was carrying on the floor. "I've been so excited about your idea of using Christmas lights. It's going to be beautiful."

I glance back at the boys who are gathering the abandoned bags.

"She's not kidding," Ryan says behind us. "She purchased every single box of lights in southern Minnesota."

Josie unhooks her arm from mine. "Well, at least we got a good deal on them since they were all in the after-Christmas sale aisles. Besides, they won't go to waste. I can always use them next year."

Liz nods, her eyes dancing with amusement. "If you use them all, it won't be hard to find you next Christmas. Your house will be visible from the space station."

Josie grins and shakes her head, her light-brown hair fanning her back. As we start unloading the bags, she shares her decorating ideas with me.

Reid pulls out a plastic container and peels back the lid. "How thoughtful, you brought food."

"I wish we had thought of that," Liz says. "Your mom sent those with us."

Ryan snatches one of the muffins. "Moms are the best."

The simple statement is like a punch to the gut. I suddenly miss my mom so much it physically hurts. I feel Reid's concerned gaze. Hoping no one has noticed our reactions, I dig further into the bag in front of me and pull out a stack of white construction paper. "What's this for?"

Josie's eyes light up. "I thought it would be fun to make paper snowflakes."

Liz laughs. "We haven't made those in years!"

"Right? Wouldn't they look perfect dangling from the ceiling?" Josie gestures around the room.

I reach into the bag again and pull out one of many light-blue plastic table coverings. "You could also place a few at the center of each table. The white snowflakes on top of the blue tablecloths would look pretty."

Liz smiles. "That's a great idea!"

Josie taps another bag. "I also have a bunch of fake, battery-operated candles to cozy up the atmosphere."

"That all sounds exceptional, but what do you want us to do?" Reid asks.

Ryan, who's devoured his muffin, wipes his hands on his jeans. "While I can make paper snowflakes as well as the next guy, surely you have a better use of our brawn."

Josie giggles at her boyfriend. "Your *brawn*?"

He flexes his bicep, but his sweater conceals any muscles he might possess.

Liz pats Ryan's shoulder. "Wow. Impressive, McNaulty. You better leave the heavy lifting to Reid."

Ryan's eyes narrow. "Watch it, or I'll show Cole the picture of you wearing the school's mascot costume."

Before I can ask who Cole is, diminutive Liz's playful yet wicked glare somehow causes tall, athletic Ryan to raise his hands in surrender.

"You...wouldn't...*dare*." If there'd been a single sibilant sound in those words, Liz's response would have been a hiss.

"Fine. This time." Ryan shifts his gaze to me. "Fair warning, Em. Beware. Liz's ability to hold a grudge is legendary."

Watching the interaction between the four friends fills me with a mix of emotions—amusement, envy, and sadness.

Josie lifts one of the boxes of white lights from a bag. "I've got a project that won't tax your strength. I'd love for you guys to figure out how to string these along the deck and down to the dock."

Reid takes the box from her. "I think there are some planter hooks outside the lodge and on the light pillars. We just need a ladder and a few extension cords."

"I think the ladder is in the library. Dad was changing some of the light bulbs in there," I offer.

Reid nods. "I can grab that if you'll get some of the extension cords in that storage room behind the front desk."

We turn in different directions to accumulate the needed items. Zuri looks from me to Reid, then follows him—the traitor. I know my dog well. She's counting on Reid giving her another rawhide bone if she tags along with him.

I exit the dining room, suddenly thankful I've been included in this activity. While exploring the hidden passageway with Reid would have been nice, being part of a group again feels fantastic. I root around in the storage room, gathering all the extension cords I can find. Bringing Josie's vision to life will require as many as possible. While I'm at it, I grab a few other items that might come in handy, such as duct tape, hooks, and a screwdriver.

Both arms laden with supplies, I make my way back toward the dining room. Before I get to the entrance, things start to feel like they're slipping from my grasp, so I stop to readjust the load.

That's when I hear them.

"So, it's just her and her dad?" Josie's voice carries around the corner.

I edge closer to listen in.

"Yeah," Reid answers.

Liz's voice is next. "I saw the look you gave her when Ryan mentioned your mom. Did something happen to her mom? Are her parents divorced?"

"I don't know," Reid replies. "Whatever happened, I don't think it was that long ago. She still seems pretty devastated."

I lean my head back against the wall. I can't believe they're talking about me. Should I sneak out and leave?

"Aren't you curious?" Josie presses.

"Of course I am," Reid answers. "But I figure she'll open up when she's ready."

So much for trying to pretend all is well. He's known all along that something is wrong. Obviously, I'm not as good an actress as Josie and Liz. *Thank you, Reid, for not pushing me.*

"Well, I'm glad she's helping us," Josie says. "I like her."

Her words ease my worry.

"And who knows," Liz adds. "Maybe we can help her in some way."

"Absolutely," Josie agrees.

If only they could.

"I don't know." Ryan's hesitant voice brings back the sense of foreboding.

I brace myself for whatever he's about to say.

"She seems cool, but something doesn't seem quite right with her."

I close my eyes and hold my breath. Here it comes. Ryan's seen through my "normal girl" façade and is about to turn my one friend, Reid, against me.

"I'm just saying…." Ryan sounds a little defensive. Is someone giving him a hard look? "There must be something wrong with her if she's hanging out with the likes of you."

They all start laughing, and I can't help but smile. I push away from the wall. No more hiding.

"Hopefully, this will be enough," I call out, announcing my presence before rejoining my new friends.

Chapter II

Somehow, by Saturday afternoon, we have actually finished Josie's decoration to-do list. While Ryan and Reid return all the tools to where we found them, Josie, Liz, and I lounge on the floor of the library, enjoying a cozy fire. Our backs rest against the sofa as we make our final paper snowflakes.

Liz groans as she leans her head back to rest against the velvety sofa cushion. "I may be too exhausted to even attend this party tonight."

Josie gives her friend a gentle nudge with her elbow. "You'll perk up when *Cole* shows up."

There's that name again. This time I have the chance to ask. "Who's Cole?" I snip off a corner of my folded paper triangle.

"Her new boyfriend," Josie sings in answer. "You'll never guess where they met."

I try to think of the most random scenario possible while recognizing my relief at the fact that she has a boyfriend. That means she isn't interested in Reid. "Skydiving in the Alps?"

"Close," Josie replies.

Liz rolls her head to the side to stare at her best friend. "In what world is that close?"

Josie lowers her handiwork and lets out an exasperated sigh. "How is it not close? Both are exciting vacation destinations."

Liz looks at me with a roll of her eyes. "We met after Christmas on a Caribbean cruise."

I lower my paper. "Sounds like an interesting story. Very romantic."

A smile slides onto Liz's face. "I'll admit it was pretty special. But if you like adventure with your romance, you need to hear about how Josie and Ryan got together."

Josie unfolds her paper, revealing a beautiful symmetrical snowflake. "Our stories will have to wait for another day. We need to start getting ready for the party."

Liz opens her snowflake and lets out a sigh. "I can't tell you how happy I am that we don't have to drive home and back here again. I'm not sure I could keep my eyes open. Thanks for letting us get ready at your place, Emerson."

When I heard how far they live from here, I made the offer. Although, after the words escaped my mouth, I worried my generosity would bring back too many memories of getting ready with my sisters and cousin for various family events. But Josie and Liz didn't notice my hesitation and loved the idea, so there was no going back.

After one last snip, I unfold my snowflake. "It'll be fun." I survey the unique design that emerges. "Besides, I should be thanking you for including me in this party planning. Not everyone is as welcoming to new people as you two are."

"Aww, thanks! We try to be." Josie stands, sending small scraps of white paper fluttering off her sweater.

Liz hands her decoration to Josie and begins gathering all the bits of snowflake-falloff that scatter the floor. "Believe it or not, Lake Forest High School has only recently become welcoming, thanks to Josie and Ryan. It used to be one of the most cliquey places around, but those two had this crazy vision to make it more inclusive for everyone. I never thought it possible, but their idea is actually working."

Josie reaches out to take my snowflake. "Yeah, if you ever get tired of online school, we'd love to have you join us."

After we finish tidying up the library, my new friends head back to the dining room. I watch them walk away, wondering if I'll ever be able to attend school in person again.

~

The plan was to quickly change and head back to the lodge to ensure everything is set before the youth group members start arriving. We should have known our plan had zero chance of succeeding because three teenage girls getting ready together is never a quick process—sharing one bathroom, one mirror, one curling iron, not to mention all the laughter. Needless to say, no way were we going to make our scheduled meeting time with the guys. Hopefully, they were managing on their own.

Deciding on what to wear consumes more brain power than I'd like to admit. Even though I won't be skating, it's an outdoor party, so I'll need layers to stay warm. Since I'll be meeting new people, looking cute is my top priority. I was able to find thermal long johns and thick woolen leggings to wear overtop. Those will be practical yet somewhat stylish paired with my thickest long sweater. All day, I've been unsure and questioning the decision. Now, Liz and Josie's similar outfits ease my mind. I certainly don't want to be the weird, new girl that doesn't fit in.

While we're reassuring each other that we all look adorable, Dad knocks on my door. I slide off my bed and open it.

He's standing there with a smile on his face. But as his gaze shifts and he takes in the chaos of the room and the sight of three girls dolled up for the evening, his expression changes. His eyes cloud over, and his hand covers his mouth. He doesn't often discuss the past, but seeing the three of us must bring back the same memory I've been wrestling with all evening.

A few years ago, we went to New York City on a family trip. Dad had booked a two-bedroom suite. The night we were going out on the town to see a Broadway show, my sisters and I were trying to get ready in our one room, which resulted in a comedic scene that elicited as many laughs as the stage production we saw. Clothes were tossed everywhere as we primped amid endless giggles.

Standing in the cabin's hallway, Dad regains his composure. "You all look fantastic. I think the three young men at the door will agree."

"The guys are here?" Josie asks in surprise.

We were so busy chatting, we didn't even hear the knock on the cabin door.

Liz takes a step forward. "Did you say *three?*"

Dad nods, and she squeezes past him, disappearing in a flash.

Josie looks at me and places her hand over her heart. "Aww…young love. She hasn't seen Cole in at least a week."

Josie, Dad, and I join the others in the cabin's small living room. Liz has launched herself into Cole's arms—a move I would have expected from the free-spirited Josie, not so much the more reserved Liz.

From the name, I'd pictured Liz's boyfriend to be blond-haired and blue-eyed. But Cole is a tall, athletic-looking guy with dark hair and olive skin. He looks to be of Middle Eastern or Spanish descent. They make a cute couple.

"Sorry it took us so long to get ready." Josie shuffles around Liz and Cole in our cozy cabin. "We better head to the lodge and finish preparing before everyone else arrives."

Ryan reaches out, expertly guiding her around the mantle of the stone fireplace, keeping her from hitting her head on it. "No worries. We already took care of it."

Josie's eyes light up. "You're a keeper, McNaulty."

The space seems to shrink around us amid the flurry of activity as Josie, Liz, and I pull on our hats, mittens, scarves, boots, and coats. The two couples and Reid pile out the door, making the space seem infinitely larger.

I stretch up on my tiptoes to kiss Dad's stubbly cheek. "I hope you're not too lonely tonight."

He grins. "I've got Zuri to keep me company." His eyes well up once again. "Have fun tonight, okay?"

"I will."

Once I join my friends on the porch, we make our way toward the lodge. This time we walk past the pathway leading to the side entrance so we can enter from the large front doors.

Reid slows his pace, allowing the two of us to lag a little behind the others. "I brought you a few things."

My heartbeat quickens. "Like what?" A girl could get used to his surprises.

He holds up the bag he's carrying. "Some hand and foot warmers. And I bought you a new scarf."

I pat my fuzzy scarf with a mittened hand. "I already have several, but thanks."

"This one has a battery-operated heater to keep you warm."

All these warming devices may not be needed, as his thoughtfulness does the trick heating my insides. "Thank you. That's so sweet."

He shrugs it off like it's no big deal. "I want you to enjoy yourself. And you have made it quite clear just how cold you get."

I nudge him with my shoulder.

The wide, elegant exterior staircase leads us toward the warm glow of light from the lodge's front windows. What a beautiful welcome. Ryan and Cole pull open the doors, letting the rest of us experience the lodge's grandeur the way it was meant to be seen. And it doesn't disappoint. The place is gorgeous. All creepiness has been swept away with the dust. Warm lights enhance the polished wood floors, making them glow.

In awe, we continue through the entryway to the dining room. I gasp. Beside me, Josie squeaks, and Liz sucks in a breath. The room we left an hour ago now shimmers and shines amid glowing candles and twinkling lights.

Reid laughs at our reactions. "If you think this looks good, just wait till you see the back deck."

He leads us through the French doors to the deck. Strands of Christmas lights flow from the lodge, along the railings, down the wooden steps, and all the way to the frozen lake. Adjacent to the dock, the gazebo—so pretty even in the daytime—now looks like something from a fairy tale. At the base of the deck, off to the right, a large firepit has been uncovered from the mounds of snow. Inviting benches surround a roaring fire. Music playing from giant speakers at the base of the steps adds the perfect touch to the shimmering lights, the twinkling stars, and the glistening snow.

"What do you think?" Reid asks me.

I look at him in amazement. "It's magical." Our eyes lock, and the beautiful scene around us seems to disappear.

I'm unaware that the others have joined us until Josie's squeal breaks the special moment.

"This is so amazing!" She latches onto Reid's arm. "Thank you so much for offering to host this skating party."

Liz slowly turns in a circle, taking in all the details. "When you suggested it, I had no idea it would be like this."

And to think, I almost convinced myself to stay home and miss it all.

We return to the dining room, and before long, the rest of the youth group and the two young adult leaders start to arrive. Reid is the perfect host and makes a point of introducing me to everyone. As nice as they all are, I doubt I'll ever see them again, so I don't pay much attention to their names. The chances of Dad and I staying here for very long are pretty slim, not to mention that as much as I enjoy hanging out with Reid and his youth group friends, I'm still not feeling ready to jump back into the whole church thing. Mom would be devastated if she knew, but my faith in every institution has taken a hit.

"We'd love to have you join us," Matt, the youth group leader, tells me when I meet him.

I don't know if his wife, Tori, can sense my hesitation, but she quickly speaks up. "No pressure. We're pretty laid back and welcoming. Just ask Liz. She only recently joined."

"Really? I didn't realize that." I glance toward my new friend, who's standing in a group, chatting like she's been part of the church group her entire life.

Reid nods. "Josie's been inviting her for years, and she finally started coming after the holidays."

"Well, think about it." Tori's warm smile demands one in return. "And in the meantime, enjoy the party."

"Thanks."

Matt puts his arm around his wife, and they walk away, leaving Reid and me alone.

"So." I can't quite read his grin. "Ready to go skating?"

I shake my head. "I don't have skates, remember?"

His smirk turns into a little-kid-trying-to-keep-a-secret smile. "Well, I took it upon myself to remedy that situation. My mom said you could borrow her skates for the evening."

I gape at him. The thoughtfulness of this family leaves me at a loss for words.

"I promise, you're in good hands," he assures me.

I bite my lower lip, gaining my composure. "You're not going to take no for an answer, are you?"

"Nope."

"Well, I would like to try out my new heated scarf and these nifty hand and foot warmers."

We pile back into our accessories—my neck, hands, and feet toasty warm. Then Reid grabs a bag and leads me out the French doors and down to the frozen lake. We stop at a bench, and he pulls two pairs of ice skates from the bag. I slide my feet from the warm cocoon of my boots and slip them into the skates. He helps me lace them, and soon, we're geared up and ready to go.

He reaches out a gloved hand, and I place my furry mitten on top. I stand, facing our icy destination, and cling to him for support as I take a few tentative steps, on wobbly ankles, toward the frozen lake. I'm just starting to get my balance when we reach the lake. Staring at the icy expanse, I begin to rethink the wisdom of this plan.

Reid notices my hesitation. "Trust me."

His eyes have a hypnotic effect and I acquiesce with a nod.

He turns toward me with a smile and reaches out his other hand, which I gladly grasp, needing all the help I can get. Then he takes a step backward onto the ice and, with a confident look, encourages me to join him.

Pushing the nerves away, I move forward, the blade of my skate touching down on the ice. I gingerly step forward with the other foot. When I'm completely on the frozen lake, Reid beams and slowly starts moving backward, pulling me along.

"You've got this." His reassurance almost makes me believe it.

Realizing I'm bent over like a little old lady, I straighten. Reid must think the movement means I'm ready for the next step of this lesson because he drops one of my hands so we can both face forward. The lack of contact on that one hand sends a surge of panic through me.

"Ready to go nice and slow?" he asks.

"Is there an option B, like I sit and watch you skate?" My question is muffled by the heavy scarf.

I cling tightly to his hand and watch how the other skaters effortlessly glide across the ice.

Someone has wisely placed traffic cones and caution tape on the lake to keep people from venturing too far away from the lodge. The makeshift barrier creates a circular rink. After about three turns around the circle, my confidence grows, and I ease up on my grip.

"Thanks," Reid says. "I didn't want to say anything, but you were kinda cutting off my circulation."

With my other hand, I playfully shove his chest, but the movement causes me to lose my balance, and the flailing begins. Reid widens his stance and somehow keeps us both upright.

"You all make it look so simple," I tell him when I'm steady again.

He laughs. "It wasn't always that way. Raina and I didn't learn to ice skate until we moved here. Like you, we were overwhelmed by the long, cold winters. Mom got tired of dealing with two kids cooped up in a house all day, and quickly discovered the importance of indoor activities—malls, rec centers, and our favorite, the indoor ice rink."

As we near the back of the designated skating area, I look toward the lodge and all the glimmering lights. "You really did an amazing job with this party. The lodge is stunning."

He follows my gaze. "It did turn out better than expected. But I certainly can't take the credit. Josie had the vision. And you all helped set it up." He faces me and grins. "You're doing so well. Time for a spin."

I smile back, and then his words register. "What? No!"

Before I can protest further, he reaches across my body and takes my free hand. I'm expecting him to twirl me like on the dance floor, but instead, we skate together in a tight circle. The music wafts through the air, and I let my fears and worries disappear into the cold, crisp evening. I put all my trust into this handsome guy as he expertly guides me around the lake. I'm sure I'll pay the price tomorrow for living in the moment, but for now, I push aside my guilt and let myself be caught up in the beauty of the night, enjoying every second.

The hours pass much too quickly, filled with laughter, skating, food, games, and a quick inspirational talk about focusing on Christ in the New Year. As Matt, the youth group leader, speaks, I wonder if anyone is aware that a hypocrite sits in their midst. His words pull at my stubborn resolve but aren't quite enough to untether my protective barrier.

After all the others leave, Josie, Cole, Liz, Ryan, Reid, and I are left with the cleanup. But even this chore is enjoyable as we relive the fun of the evening while we work. No one can bring themselves to take down the sparkling lights, so we leave them up. Too quickly, we finish our tasks, and it's time for the magical night to end.

Josie wraps me in a hug before she and Liz leave with their boyfriends. "Don't be a stranger. Think about joining our youth group, okay?"

"And if we don't see you before, we'll see you at the talent show," Liz adds.

Josie nods. "You said you'd come, and we're holding you to that promise."

"I wouldn't miss it," I assure them.

Like an old married couple, Reid and I stand at the top of the porch and wave goodbye to our friends.

As the taillights of Ryan's SUV grow smaller, we step back inside the warm lodge. Reid shuts the door and turns to look at me. "I hope you had a good time."

"I really did. Thank you for inviting me."

"Well, now that the party is over, we can focus again on what other mysteries this old place is hiding."

I stifle a yawn. "Yes, but I think it will have to wait until another day."

We gather our coats and extinguish the lights as we exit the building. Reid locks the door behind us. All's quiet except for the crunch of our boots on the snow as he walks me to my cabin.

"Is it just me, or is it even colder than usual?" It's not a far walk, but my face begins to feel numb.

Reid glances at the sky. "Yeah, feels like we're in for some snow."

More snow? Why couldn't Dad and I have moved to somewhere less arctic?

When we reach my cabin, I turn to thank Reid for walking me home, but the look in his eyes stops me from saying anything. Somehow, the impossible happens yet again as my insides flood with warmth.

Just when I think he might lean in and kiss me, Reid reaches out and squeezes my mittened hand. "You better get inside before you freeze. I'll see you soon."

"Bye." The one word is all I'm able to mutter.

He walks away, and I ascend the porch steps to enter the warm cabin. Dad must have already gone to bed since only Zuri is waiting up for me. She remains curled in a ball in front of the fireplace but lifts her head. I'm grateful for the solitude because if Dad were awake, I'm not sure he'd believe my flushed cheeks are only from the bitter cold.

Chapter 12

Reid's weather prediction was correct. I wake to three new inches of powder and the sound of Dad shoveling the snow covering our porch steps. If it had been a more substantial storm, maybe I could've talked him out of attending Mass, but I know it's a futile mission, so I push myself out of bed to get ready for church.

Today, when we enter the tiny church, fewer people turn to stare at us. Several parishioners even welcome us after Mass. The small-town rumor mill must have been buzzing all week. By now, everyone within a ten-mile radius knows who we are.

Dad has always liked routines, so it's no surprise that we once again head to the B&B for breakfast. Today's special is Mabel's award-winning biscuits and gravy.

As we wait for our meals to arrive, I sip my cocoa, while Dad savors his coffee.

"So…" Dad breaks the amiable silence. "Last night was a success?"

I set down my mug, keeping my cold hands wrapped around it. "Yep. It was a lot of fun."

Dad clears his throat—a sure sign I'm not going to like whatever he's about to say. "It was great to hear you girls laughing in your room. I've really missed that."

I squirm in my seat. "Me, too."

"I'm glad you're making friends."

"They're not my friends, Dad. They're Reid's friends."

"Well, if you continue hanging out with Reid, you'll be seeing them more often." He raises the mug of steaming coffee to his lips in a pretend-casual move.

At least I now know the subject he's trying to broach—Reid. He wants me to make friends but not a boyfriend. "Dad, Reid is just a nice guy who needed some help with his party. He'll soon be busy doing whatever it is he usually does."

His eyes narrow. "Em, it's okay for you to be enjoying yourself. They would want you to. It's just that—"

"I know!" I don't mean to snap, but I do…and with more venom than necessary. I glance around the room to see if anyone is within earshot, but no one seems to be paying attention to us. I lower my voice. "It's just that it would be better if I don't get too close to anyone—especially a boy, right? You don't have to remind me."

Dad's jaw twitches as he looks out the window. His gaze drifts back to me. "This has all been extremely hard on you. I know that. I just want you to be careful."

Frustration rises like the steam drifting off my cocoa. "You think I'm stupid enough to make the same mistake twice?"

"Em, I'm only trying to protect you." He rubs his face with his left hand. Light glints off the wedding band he refuses to take off.

My dad—my rock—has endured so much because of me. I push down my misguided anger, try to squelch the overwhelming guilt, and force a small smile onto my face. "I know."

~

We pull off the main road and onto the long drive to the lodge at the same time as Reid's family, coming from the opposite direction. They follow us down the lane and pull into their driveway. Dad and I drive a bit further to our cabin. When I climb out of the truck, I notice Reid walking toward us. Without looking at my dad, I feel his pointed gaze. With no competition, Dad finally ends his one-sided stare down, turns, and heads inside the cabin. I lean against the truck. My insides spasm as Reid draws closer.

"Hey," I call out.

"Hey. How was church?"

"Excellent. I'm pretty sure there were less people dozing during the homily today. How was your Mass?"

He grins. "Great. The youth group was still buzzing about how much fun they had last night."

"It was an amazing night." So good that thinking about it still makes me smile.

He holds my gaze. "It sure was."

My cheeks tingle. Hopefully, my blush isn't noticeable since my face is already red from the cold.

His eyes shift to the cabin's front window. Could he also be wondering if my dad is watching us?

"So, are you doing anything special today?"

I tap my chin with my gloved finger and look up at the sky. "Let's see…would you consider giving Zuri a bath or finishing a crossword puzzle special?"

He lets out an exaggerated sigh. "Sounds like your day is booked solid. Guess I'll have to explore on my own."

"Hold on. You said nothing about exploring. That changes everything. I could probably squeeze you in between everything else." I smile, anxious to hear the plan. "What did you have in mind?"

"Well…" He cocks his head to the side and flashes a mischievous grin like he's got a secret he can't wait to share. "I keep thinking about the note you found."

"Me too."

"I'm pretty sure I know what the drop point is referring to."

Now he has my complete attention…not that he didn't already. "Really?"

He nods. "I can tell you about it, but I thought it would be more fun to show you." His devilish grin intrigues me.

"Let me guess. Another secret room in the lodge?"

He shakes his head. "Nope. It's on the property, but we will have to travel to get there."

"Oh, okay. Let me change, then we'll drive there."

His mischievous smirk deepens. "I have a better idea. Let's snowshoe instead."

When my mouth drops open, he laughs.

"Not a fan of snowshoeing?"

"I don't know. I've never tried it."

"Well, are you game to try another new winter sport?" He arches an eyebrow. "Unless you're too scared."

"Challenge accepted." I manage to inject more confidence into my voice than I actually feel.

"Great. Get some warm clothes on, and I'll be back in about twenty minutes." He turns and walks away.

I watch him stride toward his house. How on earth did he just get me to agree to spend more time than I need to in this bitter cold? He must possess some magical powers. *Who am I kidding? An afternoon alone with Reid is worth the risk of hypothermia.*

I quickly change into my snow gear, adding the battery-operated scarf and placing hand and foot warmers inside my gloves and boots. By the time I'm good to go, Reid is knocking at my door. Zuri eagerly watches my face to see if she can join the adventure.

I manage to squat down, despite all my layers, and give her a hug. "I'm sorry, you can't come this time." She whines in protest. I look at Dad, who's leaning against the kitchen door jamb. His silence speaks volumes.

"We're just doing a little snowshoeing," I assure him. "I'll be back in a while."

He lets out a grunt and consents with a barely perceptible nod. I open the door, anxious to flee my moody roommates and their piled-on guilt for leaving them for Reid.

He's already waiting, sitting on the bottom step of our porch. I join him, and he shows me how to secure the snowshoes to my boots.

I play it cool for a while, but the suspense is killing me. "So, can you tell me about this mysterious place?" I stand and take a few cautious steps, trying to get used to the contraptions strapped to my feet.

"It's a small, rustic cabin that Raina and I discovered this summer."

I want to ask more, but plodding across the plowed parking lot takes coordination and concentration. My inquiring mind is eager to discover more about the mentioned cabin, but our easy journey abruptly ends at a tall wall of snow. Climbing to the top of the snowbank is a challenge, even for Reid with his long legs. At the summit, he turns and gives me a hand. Ungracefully, I scramble up and manage to stand. While I don't stay completely on top of the snow, I don't sink all the way through, either. These snowshoes are pretty handy devices.

I follow in Reid's footsteps, but even with the easier pathway, moving forward is slow-going and tiresome. Despite the frigid air, I'm soon quite warm from the exertion and turn off the heated scarf to keep from sweating.

After a few more feet, my legs need a break. "Hold up, I need to rest a minute."

He gives me a concerned look. "You doing okay?"

"I had no idea this was so much work." I take a deep breath and finally take in the view.

In order to avoid tripping over the snowshoes and falling face-first in the snow, I've been laser-focused on staying in Reid's foot-steps, and not even aware of the scenery. The picturesque lake is on our right. The sun has burned off the clouds, and the solid ice surface now shimmers under its radiant rays. I gaze back toward the welcoming lodge, dock, and gazebo, drinking in the view

"It's beautiful out here."

He turns to take in the sight as well. "Yeah, it really is. This is the view that captivated my mom."

"You said you and Raina weren't sure about moving here?"

He nods, then gives a half-shrug. "We liked the idea of living here, but didn't want to be so far away from our friends. For me, though, it didn't take long to discover how much I love solitude. I had no idea I was an outdoorsy guy."

I smile at him. "It suits you well."

"Of course, it's not like I lived in a major city. For most of my life, we lived in Lake Forest, which is not exactly a booming me-tropolis." He tilts his head and abruptly switches the focus of the conversation. "What about you? Do you prefer city life or being here in the boonies?"

I carefully choose my words. "I've never lived in a big city, either, but I've always enjoyed visiting them."

He grins. "You just wish for one a little further south."

"You've got me figured out. Although, I think I've discovered the key to surviving this cold. Raising your body temperature by snowshoeing everywhere—it's exhausting!"

"We're about halfway there. Think you can make it?"

"Lead the way."

Every few steps, I daydream about relaxing in a hot bubble bath tonight where I can soothe my sore muscles. Visualizing the pampering treat helps me keep moving until, not realizing that Reid has stopped, I plow right into him. My face barrels into his solid back. "Oof!"

He tries to take a step forward, but with my snowshoe on top of his, he loses his balance. He grabs my arm, but his attempt to steady himself results in both of us falling into the snowdrift. We look at each other and simultaneously burst into laughter. I try to push myself up, but my fist sinks into the snow, leaving me stranded. The failed move makes us laugh even harder. Soon, tears stream down my face.

"Uh oh," Reid mutters through gasps of breath as he tries to calm himself. "Watch those tears. They may freeze, leaving icicles dangling from your cheeks." He snickers, obviously imagining the sight.

I do too, and the image amps up the frenzy. Soon, my sides ache from laughter.

When we finally get ourselves under control, I roll my head in his direction. "Wow, I haven't laughed that hard in so long."

He gives me a brisk salute. "Glad to be of service."

After another unsuccessful attempt to push myself up, I flop back, exhausted from the effort. "All right, I give. How do we get ourselves out of this predicament?"

He pulls off one of his gloves so he can wipe his eyes, then slides his hand back in. "There's only one thing to do in such a situation."

I listen carefully, ready to follow his instructions.

He throws his arms out to the side. "We make snow angels." He grins, then proceeds to do exactly that.

I laugh, watching him slide his arms and legs through the snow. "In our house, they are known as snow princesses." I push aside the memory of doing this with my sisters last winter and join in the childhood game, although moving my legs with the snowshoes attached makes the effort more challenging.

Finally, using all his core strength, Reid gets himself to a standing position and reaches out a hand to me. I'm tempted to pull him back down in the snow, but I'm afraid we may never get up again, so I let him extract me from the soft powder.

We stand for a moment and admire our angel patterns. I pull out my phone to capture the image and solidify the memory.

"Can you send that to me?" he asks.

"Sure, but I don't have your number."

As he rattles it off, I type it in. The task doubles my phone contacts, as Dad's number has been the only one programmed into my new phone.

I shove the device back in my pocket and return my hand to the warmth of my mitten. "Hopefully, that cabin is close."

"Well, before you threw us into the snow, I was about to say 'we're here.'"

All I see are more mounds of snow and dark green trees. I breathe in their piney scent. Reid shuffles forward, and I dutifully follow. Within a few steps, a wooden structure, previously hidden by a thick grove of trees, comes into view.

Reid stops next to the little cabin. "Raina and I thought this was some kind of storage space or old fishing shack. But after reading the note you found, I'm wondering if this is the drop point that was mentioned. It would be a convenient location since it's well hidden, yet not too far from the lodge."

I run my mittened hand along the log wall. "*Drop point* is such an odd term. It sure brings nefarious activities to mind." I turn to look at him. "Shall we explore?"

He laughs. I can't blame him. Even I can hear the over-eager tone of my voice.

"Sure, although we've got a little work to do first."

We spend the next fifteen minutes shoving snow drifts away from around the door so we can pull it open.

After removing our snowshoes, Reid pushes the door open and we enter. The dingy space smells like an old shoebox and consists of only two small rooms. Both are empty except for a large wooden chest occupying one corner. I immediately move toward it. With a glance back at Reid, I slowly raise the lid and peer inside. Disappointment fills me when I see nothing but air.

"I guess assuming something would be left at the drop sight was too much to hope for." I plop down on the cold floor and lean against the chest, my weight moving it slightly.

Reid tilts his head and frowns.

I sit up straighter. "What is it?"

He drops to one knee and brushes at the floor near the chest. "Look."

I shift for a better view of whatever has captured his attention. My eyes scan the dirty floorboards. Where the chest sat before I pushed it aside, the boards are a slightly different color—not a huge surprise. I'd been amazed, when Mom insisted we move the rugs to sweep the wooden floor in our old house, how much darker the boards were that hadn't been exposed to the light.

But it doesn't make sense here. The floorboards under the chest are a lighter shade, not darker. Maybe they were never stained because of the chest? Then I pull in a sharp, quiet breath. A fine line travels through each board, like they were cut.

Before I fully understand what I'm seeing, Reid shoves the chest completely out of the way. That done, he snaps his wide-eyed gaze upward to meet my matching one. We've uncovered a trap door, long hidden beneath the old piece of furniture.

"Whoa. The drop point is hidden. Intriguing." I smile his way.

He laughs. "Nothing at all suspicious about that."

I inspect the mismatched floorboards but find no hinges or handles. "How do we open this thing?"

Reid pulls off his gloves and reaches into his coat pocket. His hand reappears, clutching a pocketknife. "We pry it open."

I watch as he slides the blade between the wooden planks and shimmies it under. Soon, the section of wood lifts up. He repockets his knife and pushes the loose floorboards off to the side. Complete darkness and stale air greet us as we peer into the hidden space. I turn on my phone flashlight, but the dim glow doesn't pierce the deep darkness.

He turns to look at me. "How daring do you feel?"

I'm torn between longing to immediately explore and wanting to return with a proper flashlight and a weapon, but one look at the challenge in his eyes leaves me only one option. "Let's do it."

One at a time, we lower ourselves into the dirt room beneath the cabin. The only things inside the cramped crawl space are a few empty crates and discarded tarps.

The cellar-like space seems innocent enough, but not the wooden stairs leading into the abyss. What had the O'Malleys been hiding? It couldn't have been legal, otherwise they would have had it delivered to the lodge.

"Hey, look. I think there's a tunnel down there." Reid is part-way down the stairs, shining his light into the darkness.

I draw closer and peer into the inky blackness. "Where do you think it goes?"

He looks back at me, his face so close my cheeks tingle with heat. "One guess."

Of course. "To the lodge."

"That's what I'm thinking. Should we turn around and come back another day?"

I nod. "Yes."

"Are we going to?"

A giggle bursts from my lips. "Probably not."

Reid turns his attention to his phone and opens his messages. "I'll send Raina a text so someone knows where to find us if something happens."

"Wise idea."

"Hey," he says as he types, "I'm not just a pretty face."

I'm glad it's dark and he's not looking at me because, this time, there is no cold wind to camouflage my blush.

With that small piece of responsibility behind us, we venture into the unknown with only the small beams of our phone lights. Reid leads the way, while I cling to the back of his jacket.

After only a few steps, I notice that it's slightly warmer down here—the soil being a natural insulator.

To avoid focusing on the creepiness of the place—and the foolishness of this outing—I start talking. "I wonder if there's any way to determine when this tunnel was made. That alone could shed a light on what they were hiding and whether they were using it for, good or bad."

"Thanks to your research, we know the family owned this land for a long time. So, it could have changed uses over the decades."

Possibilities flicker through my mind as we make our way through the tunnel, presumably to the lodge. Even though there is no heavy snow to traverse, the dark unknown keeps us moving at the pace of a sloth. Eventually, our journey ends at a rough wooden door. After Reid shoves it with his shoulder a few times, it jerks open with a loud creak.

I peer around him. We've reached a room with a bed, a large dresser, a small side table, and a gas lamp. "Looks like they were prepared to welcome unannounced guests."

"The plot thickens."

Slivers of light sneak in between cracks in the siding to brighten the musty-smelling space. Five framed, slightly crooked photographs hang above the bed. I take a closer look, while Reid scans the perimeter.

Each picture shows a man wearing a suit. They all have similar features—sandy brown hair, long, straight noses, and thick eyebrows hovering over piercing gazes. Based on the men's clothing and the photos' differing clarity, it seems the images span numerous decades. I recognize these men from my research. They are the five generations of men—the owners of the lodge and surrounding property—who all bore the same name. James O'Malley.

If only these photos could talk.

"Emerson."

I turn. Reid is standing in front of another door. As he pushes it open, an odd glow casts a sickly, green light on his face.

Curiosity pulls me from the photos.

Peering into the room, my gaze lands on the source of the unusual light. Near the top of the wall to my left is a small window with yellow and green panes of glass. An intricately carved wooden table sits below it, with a large gold cross in the center. An altar?

This new discovery confuses me even more. I'd been suspicious that these men had been up to no good. This deepens the mystery.

"Look at this."

I turn, drawn by something in Reid's voice. On the opposite side of the little room, he stares up a staircase, dimly illuminated by the light from his phone.

His eyes are lit with intrigue when he turns my way. "Think we're at the bottom of the steps you discovered the other day?"

"Probably."

Without a word, we agree on the next move. I follow him up the winding stairs.

At the first level. a door opens to the lodge kitchen's supply closet. A quick peek reveals that from inside the small room, the door looks like the innocuous back of a pantry. No one would ever suspect it was a door.

We continue up the stairs, and sure enough, end up in the narrow space behind the bedroom on the second floor where I found the note a few days ago.

"Well, I guess we've solved one mystery," Reid says. "Although, I'm not sure we'll ever know what these secret rooms and passageways were actually used for."

"Are you waving the white flag of surrender? I, for one, am not ready to give up. I think I'll do some more research tomorrow. Care to join me?"

He rakes his hand through his hair. "Wish I could. I have a meeting after school. But if you find anything interesting, keep me informed?"

I laugh. "I promise you'll be the third to know."

Chapter 13

Unsure of the greeting I'll receive after spending the afternoon alone with a boy, I slowly open the cabin door when I return. My stomach growls at the tantalizing scent wafting through the cabin—most likely from one of Mrs. Stevenson's dishes. Zuri's in front of me in two quick strides. She proceeds to whine, howl, and "talk" as she complains about her day.

"Geez." I address Dad, who's sitting in the recliner, reading his newest crime drama. "Didn't you give her any attention this afternoon?"

He looks up from his book. "She's telling you that *you* should be spending more time with her and less time with a boy."

"Oh, is that what she's saying?" I shake my head and peel away my layers. "The house smells delicious. I'm starving."

"Snowshoeing can burn a lot of calories."

His words are casual, but the concern lurking in his eyes is not. I turn away, under the guise of hanging up my coat and putting away my scarf and mittens. I know Dad's looking out for my well-being and doesn't want me to get too attached to this place, and a certain handsome boy, before we have to move once again. But can't he be happy that I'm no longer moping in my room?

Determined not to let him ruin my good mood, I curl up in the adjacent chair. "You won't believe what we discovered." As our dinner cooks, I tell him about the tunnel, the shack in the woods, and the staircase that led us to the second-story bedroom. As I talk, he lowers his book, but his expression is hard to read.

"Wow. That's quite something." He's still not revealing his thoughts.

"Guess you were right about there being more secret rooms."

His somber face finally softens. "You should listen to your wise father more often."

I smirk in response. "I wonder if that little cabin is the original homestead. Hey, can I borrow the truck to go into town tomorrow? I'd like to return the magazine Mrs. Grier lent me and see if she found anything else about the O'Malleys' property."

He shakes his head. "Sorry, kid. I have to drive out to meet with an electrician."

"Oh." Well, there goes that plan. "Then could I do some research on my laptop?" His jaw twitches, but before he can say no, I quickly add my own single-syllable word. "Please?"

He rubs his temple like I'm giving him a headache. "Em."

I slide out of my comfy seat and drop to my knees next to his chair, ready to plead my case. "Dad, I promise I'll only look up things about this property and the owners."

Despite my reassurances, his narrowed eyes and set jaw tell me he's still unconvinced. Really? I push the wave of annoyance as far away as possible. Throwing a fit won't help the situation. "You can check my search history."

"By then, it will be too late."

I sink back on my heels. "Dad, why can't you trust me?"

He studies my face for a moment, then lets out a heavy sigh and reaches out to stroke my hair. "I'm sorry, honey. I do trust you. It's just hard not to worry."

"I know." I plead with my eyes, taking advantage of his softening attitude. "But I promise I won't put us in jeopardy."

The oven timer dings. He stands and reaches out a hand to help me up. "Okay. You can surf the web. But only about the lodge and the O'Malleys." The hard lines on his face shift into a tired smile.

I wrap my arms around him and bury my face into the folds of his shirt. "Thank you. I won't let you down."

He squeezes me tight. "And while you're on there, maybe you can place an order for groceries."

~

After I finish my online classes the next day, I search for information about the O'Malleys and the lodge property. There's not much more about them than what I already discovered at the library. However, I *do* uncover some more recent history.

The property has changed ownership several times since James O'Malley's death. It sat vacant for a while before a Minneapolis mega-church bought it. They used it as a retreat center for several years until a financial scandal closed the church.

After that, the lodge became a rehab facility for a short time. The two failed attempts to revive the place fueled rumors about it being haunted.

Finally, the Stevensons became the proud owners of the lodge and the surrounding land. Hopefully they will break the pattern and be more successful than their predecessors.

Unable to find anything more, I close the laptop to find Zuri staring at me, her ears perked and eyes wide. "Okay. Ready for a walk?"

At the sound of her favorite word, she zips around the living room, making it a challenge to put on her sweater, booties, and leash. Finally, we're both ready to head outside.

Knowing Zuri needs a longer outing than usual, I guide her down the snow-packed driveway toward the road. As we near the Stevenson's home, I see Reid's car isn't parked in its usual spot. Guess he's still at his meeting. A pang of disappointment rips through me.

As we're passing the house, the front door flings open, and Raina rushes down the steps. "Hey!"

Zuri tugs forward, and I patiently wait out their reunion, complete with hugs, slobbery kisses, and high-pitched squeals from both of them.

"Hi, Raina. We haven't seen you in forever. You keep so busy."

She stands, finally acknowledging me. "I know! But today, practice was canceled. I was just thinking about walking over to your place when I saw you guys headed my way."

"Great minds think alike."

"Right? Want some company on your walk?"

"Sure. We're heading toward the road, but just so you know, neither Zuri nor I have adjusted to this cold weather, so we might chicken out at any moment."

I hand over the leash upon her request, and we continue our walk. "Just a few more months, and then it will warm up."

"*Months?*"

She laughs at my dismay. "You'll get used to the cold eventually."

I pull my scarf higher to cover my nose and mouth. "I'm not so sure about that."

"Winter isn't all bad. I heard you learned how to use snowshoes."

Concealed by my scarf, a smile forms as I think about the special afternoon spent with Reid.

"And," Raina continues, "Reid said you learned to skate."

A laugh sneaks out from amid the layers. "Well, I'm not sure you could call what I did skating—more like clinging to Reid's arm as he led me around the ice."

"Gotta start somewhere!"

"Indeed." Although we haven't quite made it to the main road—my intended destination—I'm thinking about turning back. My toes are beginning to tingle. Why hadn't I grabbed some of those handy foot warmers? "Ready to head back?"

"Sure." Her breath creates a puff of air.

We pivot to face the way we came. Zuri continues toward the road, and then dutifully follows our new direction.

"So what else have you been up to?" Raina asks.

"I've been doing research on the lodge."

"Oh, cool! Did you discover who built the hidden room?"

"Not yet. That pool room is pretty awesome, isn't it?"

"Yeah," she agrees. "But the upstairs space is the really interesting one."

Her words surprise me. "Oh, Reid told you about the second hidden door?" Of course he did, just like I told Dad.

"We discovered it together."

Her words ricochet around in my head, not quite making sense. I was the one who found the upstairs space after reading the interview with the former maid. "You mean, you two found the billiard room beside the library?"

"We found both hidden places." She lets Zuri investigate a cluster of pine trees before continuing on. "A few months ago, soon after we discovered the pool room, we were checking out all the upstairs rooms and happened to find the upstairs secret panel. It's so mysterious, isn't it?"

As we return to her house, my steps slow as realization hits.

Raina hands Zuri's leash to me. "See ya later, Emerson!" She gives Zuri one last hug, and then dashes up her front porch steps.

I'm frozen in place until Zuri pulls on the leash. My legs slowly move, weighed down with the revelation that Reid lied to me.

With each step, the stinging pain of his betrayal mounts within me. Why had he pretended he didn't know about the second false door? His cute smile had lured me in and I believed him. Why did I let myself trust him? How could I have been so stupid?

Back at the cabin, I slam the front door and peel off the layers. I turn on the fireplace, then sink down into the chair, staring at the flames. When will I learn I can't trust anyone?

I'm not sure how long I've been lost in my thoughts when Zuri leaps to her feet, staring at the front door. My human capabilities catch up to her superior canine senses as I hear the crunch of snow. Someone's approaching the cabin door. The darkness of the room startles me. How long have I been staring at the dancing flames, wallowing in self-pity? The furious wag of Zuri's tail gives me a clue to the owner of the crunchy footsteps. It has to be one of two people—Dad or Reid. And since Dad usually comes in the back door, this can only be the one person I have no desire to see.

Reid knocks on the door as Zuri whines and spins in a tight circle. I sit motionless. Should I pretend to not be home? But what's the point? This confrontation is unavoidable. Living so close to one another, it's not like I can hide from him for long. Better to get it over with.

I push myself from the comfy chair. *Here goes nothing.*

I flip on the light, the golden glow chasing away the shadows, and open the door. Reid smiles at me, and then turns his attention to the jumping canine, who—unlike me—is thrilled to see him.

After giving Zuri some love, he straightens and looks at me, his face red from the cold. "Hey, I was curious if you found any new info on the lodge."

I lean against the doorframe. "Why? Is there someplace else you'd like to pretend to be surprised about?"

His face scrunches in confusion. "What?"

His playing dumb only increases my ire. "Drop the act, Reid. I'm not interested in your little game."

He glances over his shoulder as if he thinks I'm talking to someone else. "I don't know what you're talking about."

I cross my arms, closing myself off from his excuses. "Well, let me spell it out for you. I know you'd already found the secret door in the upstairs guest room. Thanks for making me feel like an idiot."

He closes his eyes and lets out a deep breath. "Raina."

"Don't get mad at your sister for not covering up your lies." I step inside to close the door, but he sticks his foot in the opening to block the move.

"Em, it's not what you think."

He's really going to keep up the charade? I tilt my head. "Really? You weren't pretending to be surprised by the hidden room I'd found?"

His eyes hold a desperate plea. "It wasn't all a lie. I honestly didn't know about either of the hidden passageways or the note." My stony silence doesn't deter him. "Can I please come in?"

Undeterred by his smooth talk, I hold my position. "No."

He takes a step backward. His gaze travels to the ceiling of our front porch. Now that he's out of the way, I should shut the door and end this conversation. But a tiny sliver of curiosity makes me want to hear what he has to say.

"Look," he begins. "You were so sad when you first arrived, and for some reason, I wanted to make you smile. The only time you showed any emotion or interest was when you heard about the legend of the lodge. Then when you started working on the mystery of the place, you came out of your shell and revealed a little of your true self. I—I didn't want those moments to end."

His words trigger something inside me, and my anger and mistrust resurface. "You don't know anything about me." In one swift move, I slam the door in his face.

"Emerson!" he calls.

I lean against the door, tears stinging my eyes. How could I have let loneliness so cloud my judgment that I could be manipulated like that? I feel like such a fool.

Chapter 14

Luckily, either Dad realizes I'm not in the mood to chat, or he has his own problems to worry about. Whatever the reason, he doesn't ask about my quiet mood all through dinner. Thank goodness. An I-told-you-not-to-spend-so-much-time-with-the-cute-boy-next-door lecture is not what I need.

"Want to watch a show or something?" he asks as I clear the table.

"Nah, I think I'll take Zuri to the lodge. I left one of the books I was reading over there."

He nods. The sympathetic look on his face, confirms he knows I'm upset about something, and is far worse than any gloating would have been. "As long as you take Zuri and a flashlight."

I finish rinsing the dishes, then start the process of getting Zuri and myself bundled up to go outside. The laborious task has become routine.

Outside, she sniffs around for a suitable place to do her business. Then we crunch across the icy snow to the lodge, the flashlight beam scanning the area. You'd think this drafty old building, which I used to think was rather creepy, would be the last place I'd want to go tonight. But after these past few weeks, it's become like a friend you feel comfortable with and want to learn more about.

I slide the key in the lock of the side door and enter. As usual, Zuri dashes down the shadowy hallway ahead of me. My progress is slow as I turn on lights along the way. It's not until I reach the dining hall that I realize the lights are already on in the library. I peer in to see Reid crouched near the fireplace petting Zuri. Great.

I enter the room, and they both look up with expectant expressions. To make things even worse, Reid looks quite handsome in a maroon henley, which not only shows off his biceps but compliments his dark hair.

He gestures to the small fire. "It should be warm in a few minutes."

"Sorry, I didn't know anyone was here." I grab the book I came to retrieve from the side table.

Zuri gets another pat before Reid stands. "Please, don't go." He tilts his head to the left, just like Zuri. "I was actually trying to figure out how I could get you here so we could talk."

"You couldn't possibly say anything that would make things better." I pat my thigh. "Come on, Zuri, let's go."

The dog slinks toward me with her tail between her legs.

"Can you please hear me out?" he pleads.

"We have nothing to talk about."

Ignoring my words, he takes a step forward. "You were right, Emerson. I shouldn't have been deceptive. It's just that I wanted to get to know you better. Like I said, you only came alive when we were discussing the mystery surrounding the lodge. I'm sorry I didn't share that I knew about the hidden doorway you found. And yes, I'd hoped you would discover it so we'd have something to talk about. But what's the harm in that?"

I shake my head and turn to leave, too exhausted to even attempt an explanation.

"Why are you so scared to let anyone in?"

His question stops me in my tracks. "Leave it alone, Reid. You don't know anything about me."

"I think I know more about you than you realize."

Something about his statement infuriates me. I spin back toward him. "Really? And what do you think you know?" I glare at him, ready for his ridiculous theory, which I will shred apart and leave him standing in the pieces.

He squeezes his eyes shut, like he's having an internal debate. Finally, he looks at me, his intense gaze boring into mine. "I think you're in witness protection."

My breath catches. Whatever I thought he was going to say, it certainly wasn't that. "Witness protection? Seriously? You've been watching too many movies."

"I'm right, aren't I?"

I shake my head. "Reid, that's insane. I'm just a girl who has lost a lot over the last few years, and all I want is to be left alone."

But he doesn't leave me alone. He continues to talk. "From what I've gathered, you lost your mom and a sister or two."

With my free hand, I reach for the back of the nearest chair to steady myself. Hearing someone acknowledge them tears at my heart. "They're gone." The words come out in a whisper.

He steps closer, reaching for my hand. I move it before he can make contact, but he's not deterred. "But they're not dead, are they?"

I jerk my arm away before he can touch me. "I never said they were. Families fall apart for other reasons besides death."

Zuri whines, taking in our tense conversation.

"True, but divorce doesn't quite match up. You speak about them like they are gone and that you'll never see them again."

Leave, before he says anything else. I turn my back to him and start toward the door.

"Your name's not really Emerson, is it?"

I know I should keep moving, but I can't with this invisible cement holding me in place.

"And if I were to take a guess," Reid continues relentlessly, "I'd say your family was from Missouri, where one of you witnessed a horrible crime."

All moisture seeps from my mouth, leaving me unsure I'll be able to speak. I slowly look back at him. "Why would you think that?"

His warm brown eyes are pools of compassion. "I'm just putting the pieces together. You seem like you've been through some kind of trauma, but when you mention your family, it's not always in the past tense." He glances at Zuri. "You freaked when Josie called her Miss Zuri and commented that it sounded like the state."

"But jumping to such a crazy assumption of witness protection is ridiculous."

He shakes his head. "Not really. You see, one of my dad's good buddies from his military days, John, is now a federal marshal. He once told me that the witness protection program falls under their supervision. I hadn't seen him in months, but he stopped by right before Christmas. Despite the freezing weather, Dad didn't invite him inside to talk. Their body language made it clear that it wasn't a social call. He seemed to be trying to convince my dad of something. I honestly forgot about it until you and your dad showed up. Then pieces of the puzzle started to fit together."

I bite my lower lip. *Do I continue to deny it, or tell him the truth?*

He walks forward and reaches for my hand. This time, I let him grasp it. The warmth of his touch melts away the last of my defenses, and a lone tear rolls down my cheek. He pulls me to his chest and wraps his arms around me in a hug that might be the sweetest thing anyone has ever done for me.

"Reid, you can't tell anyone."

He rubs my back. "I know. But now, you can finally stop holding everything inside."

~

After the first peaceful night's sleep I've had since our ordeal began, I wake in a panic. Any good effects from having restful slumber instantly vanish. *What did I do? How could I have been so reckless?*

Tormenting thoughts fill my mind from the moment I wake. What was I thinking? Telling Reid the truth has put my whole family in even more danger. *Right?* Do I need to fess up and tell Dad? Maybe Reid won't tell anyone. He seems pretty trustworthy. *But what if he does?* The consequences are too horrific to contemplate.

Finally, in the late afternoon, when my nerves feel like they could snap at any moment, a familiar rap sounds from the front door. Reid.

With sweaty palms, I pull open the entry. One look at Reid's face is enough to melt away my worries. Those expressive eyes of his are brimming with concern.

He holds up a steaming cardboard cup that smells heavenly. "I had a feeling you might need this."

I step out of the way and motion for him to enter the cabin. "You are a mind reader."

He stomps the snow from his boots and steps inside, shutting the door behind him. "Well, about halfway through the day, I started feeling pretty guilty, so I decided to come bearing a gift."

I reach for the coffee. "Why do you feel guilty?"

His eyes narrow as he studies my face. "I figured you might be worried about having told me the truth."

A sharp laugh escapes my lips. "You really are a psychic."

His smile chases away the fears of the day. "I know it's a cliché, but I wanted to offer some assurance, Emerson. Your secret is safe with me."

I let out a slow breath. "You have no idea what a relief it is to have a friend I can talk to about it all. Dad never wants to discuss it." Realizing we're still standing in the entryway, I finally remember my manners. "Do you want to come in for a while?"

His head tilts to the side with a sheepish look. "I was actually wondering if you might like to head over to the lodge and continue our search for hidden rooms."

"That depends."

"On what?"

My eyes narrow, ready to scrutinize his answer. "Were you serious when you said that the only secret passageways you knew about were the one behind the library and the upstairs one where I found the note?"

He places his right hand over his heart. "Yes, I promise. Those are the only hidden spaces I'm aware of. The new tunnels and staircases were a complete surprise. And I'd love to keep working together to see if there are any more."

The slight plea in his voice makes me smile. "Okay. Then yes, I'd love to continue our search."

~

"What's your real name?" Reid asks as we survey the kitchen for more hidden compartments.

I hesitate, even though I know our conversation will remain private. The faint sounds of Dad hammering away on something upstairs waft into the room, and Zuri is nothing if not a trusted companion who knows how to keep secrets. But it still feels too risky to share everything. "I'm sorry, but I can't tell you. However, I will say the agents encouraged us to choose something similar to our given names so we could continue to use nicknames and not get confused or forget. Dad always called me Em, and my younger, twin sisters nicknames are El and Es. At the first place we were relocated to, I went by Emma, and my sisters chose Ella and Esme. When I came here, I chose Emerson. I'm thinking Emily, if we have to move again."

He stops his search of one of the many cupboards and looks my way. "Wait, your family was together for a while? I mean, after…you know. After whatever happened."

I nod as the painful memories resurface. "Yeah, but then we were split apart."

He leans back against the counter. "What happened?"

A deep breath pushes away the anxiety that always rushes in whenever the memory resurfaces. "I was worried about our extended family, so I tried searching for them on my laptop. When I couldn't find anything, I started scouring the news regarding the case, trying to uncover any progress the police were making. But my online searches triggered something and put us all in danger. They separated us, thinking we would be harder to track down if we weren't a family of five. My sisters went with our mom, somewhere. Dad, Zuri, and I came here."

His muscles strain against the fabric of his shirt as he crosses his arms. "Why were you searching for your other relatives? Were they also in danger?"

I nod and hop myself up to sit on the counter across from him. I ignore the nagging voice telling me not to reveal so much, because to finally share my burden feels somewhat therapeutic. "We lived in a small town. My family, my aunt and uncle and cousins, and my grandparents all lived within a few blocks of each other. We spent so much time together." The memory makes me smile. "My cousin and I are the same age and best friends. We did everything together. My grandpa liked to call us the family's partners in crime. Ironically, that proved a little too accurate. You see, it was our fault that we were all placed in protective custody." I push away that memory for the moment. "Then I made it infinitely worse. I was certain my cousin—I'll call her Keira—would have left some kind of clue to let me know she and her family were okay. I kept searching databases and online chats, but I could never figure out where they went. When my sleuthing was uncovered, Dad banned me from any more searching. But he was too late. So, you see, it's my fault that our family is in this situation and now torn apart. I don't know if we'll ever be together again."

I bury my head in my hands, hoping to stop the threatening tears. Steady arms envelop me into another hug, and suddenly, every sense is triggered. The woodsy scent of Reid's soap fills my nose, and the softness of his shirt makes me want to hold tight and never let go.

"Let's pray about it."

I draw away in reaction to the unexpected words. "I know you want to help, but there's nothing anyone can do."

He steps back as he reads my hesitant expression. "Prayers can help."

I shake my head. "They didn't help when I begged God to make the whole situation go away, or when I pleaded for our family to stay together."

He gives me the strangest look. "Em, you know that's not how prayers work, right? Bad things happen in this life. God doesn't just snap His fingers and make things better. When we face trials, He wants us to turn to Him. He can give us strength to get through the difficult times. And He can offer us wisdom to solve our problems. He's watching over your family during this time of separation. Trust Him."

I shrug. While his speech is passionate, I'm not quite buying what he's selling. "My mom used to say things like that when this whole nightmare first began. My sisters and I clung to that hope. But things didn't get better. They got worse. We were told the separation would be temporary but how can they promise that? What if I never see them again?"

He considers my words for only a moment before responding. "Your mom sounds very wise. But, even if she and I are both wrong, it doesn't hurt to try praying, right?"

His expression makes it clear that there's no use in arguing with him. "Fine."

He reaches for my hands. The warmth of his touch makes it hard to concentrate when he begins praying. "Dear Lord, we don't know why bad things happen to good people, but we know that You can bring good out of even the darkest times. Thank You for making sure Emerson's family is safe and protected. Thank You for placing her here, so that she can begin to heal surrounded by new friends who care about her. We trust that You can do anything, so we ask for Your help in this difficult situation and that this family can one day be together again. We pray this in the name of the Father, the Son, and the Holy Spirit."

Our hands slide apart as we both make the sign of the cross. His prayer lingers in my mind. I've never thought about the situation like that before. He's right. My family might be separated, but they are all safe. That is definitely something to be thankful for.

Chapter 15

Keira,

You will probably never read this. Either we will never be reunited, or when we finally are together again, I'll want to share all this with you in person. I can picture us lying side by side, like we used to do during our sleepovers, talking for hours as we catch up on what has happened since we were last together.

My dad would most likely be mad if he knew I was doing this, but Reid suggested that putting my thoughts on paper might somehow be healing. I avoided the suggestion for a while, but in the hopes of squelching the anxiety that never seems to leave, I decided to give it a try.

Your first question is probably, who's Reid? Glad you asked. He's the son of the man my dad now works for. You won't believe this, but he somehow figured out our secret. I know I shouldn't have confided in him, but it's amazing having someone I can share this burden with. There's no way you would know this, but El, Es, and my mom have been separated from us. Now it's just me and Dad, and he doesn't want to discuss things—at least, not like I do.

Anyway, back to Reid. I'm afraid I'm starting to fall for him. Yes, it's a problem since I don't know how long we'll be here. But it's not like I can just turn off my feelings. Ugh. So complicated.

You would absolutely love where we are living. Dad was hired to fix up this cool old lodge. Not only is it nestled along a beautiful lake, but Reid and I have discovered a bunch of secret passageways. I've been researching the place but haven't found an explanation as to why the hidden rooms were created or by whom. Anyway, it's been fun exploring the lodge with Reid. Our dads have even asked us to help them update the blueprints, which means we've been spending even more time together over the last few weeks. No complaints from this girl!

I told you that Reid figured out why Dad and I are here, but I haven't shared any of the details with him. I think he knows it's best if he doesn't ask too many questions, and he probably doesn't want to push me to talk about things I'm not ready to discuss. But I'm starting to wonder if opening up might be exactly what I need in order to move on. Risky I know. But ever since Reid found out what happened, I keep thinking about that night and find myself wanting to hash it out. Oh, how I wish you and I could have had a chance to dissect our memories together. Maybe there is some detail that could make all of this end soon.

Miss you and love you,
Em

I close my notebook, hiding away the letter that will never be sent or read. Reid was right. Committing my thoughts to paper somehow makes me feel less weighed down by the past.

"There you are, Emerson."

I look up to see Mrs. Grier walking toward me, carrying a cobalt blue mug. I was finally able to borrow Dad's truck so I could return the magazine she loaned me. The lure of surrounding myself with hundreds of books was too great to ignore, and I had found a cozy corner in the library to write my letter.

"I thought you might still be here somewhere." She offers me the steaming mug. "I was having a cappuccino break and thought you might like one, too.

My hands circle the warm mug. "Oh, wow. Thank you so much. This is perfect."

She grins at my enthusiasm. "We don't get many customers, so I order a different drink each day to make sure Janie doesn't forget how to make them…and to ensure she looks up from her phone at least once during her shift."

I laugh, then take a sip. *Delicious.*

"I saw you and your dad at Saint Catherine's parish last Sunday," she says.

I lower the mug. "Yes, we've gone there the last few weeks. I'll have to look for you this Sunday."

She nods and leans against the nearest shelf. "Have you figured out the trick to Father's homilies?" she asks.

Besides pinching myself to stay focused? "No. What's that?"

"Close your eyes." She grins at my surprised expression. "I'm serious. His monotone delivery and his habit of reading from his notes without looking up can be very distracting, but if you close your eyes and just listen to the words, you'll find his sermons to be quite good."

Huh. "And here I thought everyone was sleeping." As they say, appearances can be deceiving. "Thanks, I'll give it a try."

"Also, I wanted to thank you for setting me straight."

"Me?" I'm confused.

"Yes. I hadn't read the magazine article before I gave it to you, but I had a chance to look at it a few minutes ago. I hadn't realized the lodge had been a rehab facility. I feel bad because I've always believed the story that it had once been an insane asylum."

"Really?" Amazing how rumors spread. Maybe if I discover all the facts about this place, I'll write an article of my own, sharing the lodge's interesting history and bringing to light the false rumors.

~

Strategically, I wait for an afternoon when I know our dads are off property for a few hours to do what I've been thinking about doing since I composed my letter to my beloved cousin.

"Reid?"

He looks up with an easy grin from jotting down our latest measurement on the copy of the blueprint his father has us working on. "Did you tell me the wrong number again?"

I pretend to gasp and act insulted. "I told you the right number last time. It's not my fault you wrote it down incorrectly." I sit on the edge of the bed that fills most of the guest room where we're currently working. "I was hoping to talk to you about something."

He spins the pencil between his fingers. "Don't tell me you're going to try and back out of attending the talent show. Josie and Liz will kill me if I don't bring you."

I tuck a strand of hair behind my ear, a nervous gesture Keira always teased me about. "I have no idea why they want me to come, but no, that's not it." I take a deep breath to gather my courage. "I want to tell you about that night."

He requires a moment to understand the gravity of what I'm saying. When he realizes what I'm talking about, he straightens, sets down his pencil, and walks toward me. "Are you sure? I admit, I'm curious. But just because I know some of your story, doesn't mean I need to know all of the details."

"I know, it's just that I feel this need to share it all. I had no idea what a toll this secret was taking on me. When you guessed about the witness protection program, it was so freeing. I'd like to share the rest."

He sits on the corner of the bed, leaving a respectable distance between us. "Nothing you say will leave this room."

I take a deep breath and then begin. "It all started innocently enough when Keira got this crazy notion that our high school football coach was dealing drugs."

His eyes narrow. "This is all about drugs?"

I shake my head. "Just let me finish. Keira's house backed up to this field. On the other side of the field was the coach's house. Keira's bedroom window was at the back of the house, with a view of the open field. She kept complaining about bright headlights waking her up at all hours of the night, shining into her room. I just laughed it off and told her to close her curtains. But she was suspicious and convinced herself that something sinister was going on. That and the fact that our crummy football team started winning made her think Coach was providing the players with performance-enhancing drugs. I didn't believe it because Coach Carter and his wife seemed so nice. Mrs. Carter had been our elementary school music teacher, and we all adored her." A sad smile crosses my face, thinking of the cute little songs she'd created for our class.

I shift on the bed and look out the window. "One night, when I was sleeping over at Keira's house, we were up late talking, as always, when headlights appeared over at the Carters' house. She convinced me that we should sneak over there and finally see what was going on. I still didn't believe her theory, but I was up for the adventure, so we snuck out."

Reid stares at me, seeming to hang on to my every word.

"As we approached the house, we could see into the family room. Coach and Mrs. Carter were sitting on the couch, and there were two strange men in the room with them. One man was sitting on a chair next to Coach and the other stood off in the distance. Even though neither man was one of the football players, we inched closer to get a better look. Coach and the man in the chair were talking, while Mrs. Carter was looking away and didn't seem to be part of the conversation. Nothing seemed suspicious, so we left."

Reid frowns, clearly not expecting such a boring story. I plow ahead. "The incident was just a totally lame adventure until Monday when it was announced at school that the Carters had died in a car crash over the weekend." The shiver that always occurs when I think of hearing that news for the first time passes down my spine. "As soon as we could, Keira and I discovered the details. The official report was that their car had plunged off a bridge at one in the morning on Sunday. But we knew that was impossible because we had seen them in their family room at that exact time.

"We immediately fessed up and told our parents about sneaking out. They didn't seem concerned, though, and told us that the precise time of death was probably hard to pinpoint. That could have been true, but the problem was that when we were back in Keira's room, laughing about our excursion, one set of headlights moved away from the house. We didn't see any other headlights before we finally went to sleep around two-thirty. Our parents agreed it was odd but pointed out that maybe there were no other headlights because of the angle of the garage, or the Carters didn't want to wake their neighbors so kept their car's lights off until they were pulling away. But a few days later, when I was watching the news with my family, things got crazy."

"What happened?" Reid's voice is little more than a whisper.

"I recognized the man who had been talking with Mr. Carter. It was the district attorney. The other man in the Carters' living room that night was also on the news, standing behind the D.A.

as he gave a press conference—his bodyguard. When I shared that bit of news with my parents, they finally agreed we should call the police. Two detectives came to our house and interviewed Keira and me. That was the scariest part. It was a classic good cop/bad cop scenario. Even though we hadn't done anything wrong, the one detective made us feel like it was our fault that Coach and his wife had died. He kept pressing us about details we knew nothing about. His partner was much nicer and attempted to get us to open up in a friendlier way. The approach didn't matter, though—we didn't have much to tell them besides who we'd seen in the Carters' family room the night they died. Two days later, we were told the entire family had to be placed in witness protection."

"So, the D.A. is corrupt?"

"Yep. From what I gathered, he's part of a large crime network. Turns out there have been numerous suspicious deaths surrounding various court cases. My theory is that those detectives both knew what was happening at the D.A.'s office. One of them is probably in on it all. Maybe the other one knew we were in danger and wanted to protect us. I just can't decide which was the trustworthy cop, and which one was on the take. Was the nice one being friendly because he genuinely cared about us, or because he wanted us to trust him and reveal all we knew? Was the grumpy one pushing us for details because he wanted to finally expose the corruption, or because he was corrupt and trying to determine how much of a threat we were to the criminal organization he was part of?

"That was one of the things I was searching for before they separated our family. I was trying to investigate the cases those detectives had been involved in to determine who was corrupt. Of course, it was stupid to think I could uncover anything, but I hated feeling so helpless and wanted to do something."

Reid nods as he listens to my armchair analysis. "Your research probably made them think you knew more than you'd admitted."

I nod.

He reaches out his hand. "Thanks for telling me."

His touch gives me the encouragement to continue. "I can't get that night out of my head. It plays in my mind on an endless loop. When we were peering into the Carters' window, Coach and the D.A. were talking intensely. Mrs. Carter just sat there, not even looking at them. I don't know if she was watching something else or didn't want to be part of whatever they were talking about. Since it wasn't the big football scandal that Keira assumed it would be, I motioned for her that we should go. Before we snuck off, Mrs. Carter suddenly stared out the window right at us. We both flinched, thinking we'd been busted even though it was dark out and she wouldn't have been able to see us." I swallow the lump in my throat. "But what if she *did* see us?"

He rubs the back of my hand. "What do you mean?"

I let out a breath. "I know it sounds crazy, but maybe she saw our reflection on something and knew someone was watching her last moments on earth." I can barely say the next sentence. "What if she was pleading for help, and we missed it?"

He studies my face for a moment. "You're feeling guilty."

My nod confirms his statement. "If we had paid attention and done something, maybe they would still be alive."

"I know this is difficult, but you can't blame yourself. You had no way of knowing they needed help."

I let out a frustrated groan. "I just wish I could talk to Keira about it. I want to know what she remembers. That's why I tried to find her online."

"I'm so sorry." He scooches closer to pull me in for a hug.

I settle into the comfort of his embrace, wishing I could stay there forever.

"Tell me about your cousin," he says.

A smile crosses my lips as I think of her. "We're the same age and both have younger siblings, so we grew up doing everything together." Still leaning against his chest, the beating of his heart against my cheek suddenly feels too intimate. I straighten and shift to sit cross-legged on the bed. He does the same, facing me.

"Because we were the two oldest grandchildren, our grandparents had us over to their house all the time. My twin sisters and Keira's little brothers were a bit of a handful when they were young, so our exile was probably meant to give our parents a break, but we loved every moment." The memories continue to pour out of me. "Our grandma was a huge reader. That's where I developed my love of books. And Grandpa, well, he loved Alfred Hitchcock movies. Keira and I spent hours watching those old films with him. We even found an online fan group for him to join: The Hitchcock Homies."

Reid grins. "Did he post much? I can't imagine my grandparents doing that."

I laugh. "Not really. He didn't seem to quite get the whole concept, although sometimes, I wondered if he was pretending so he could spend more time with us. Anyway, we'd help him post questions or comments. That's actually the site where I tried to find Keira."

His eyebrows raise. "Really?"

I nod. "I thought I'd figured out the perfect way to contact her. But she never responded. Maybe her parents banned her from the internet sooner than mine did."

"What did you post?"

"I asked which Hitchcock movie best portrayed their lives. If anyone answered *Rear Window*, I'd start up a conversation with them. I was confident I'd be able to figure out which one was Keira." His blank expression tells me he doesn't understand my brilliant plan. "Not a Hitchcock fan?"

He shrugs. "I guess not. Maybe you could enlighten me. Tell me why *Rear Window* is the key."

"The movie's premise is that the main character observes a crime by looking through a neighbor's window."

His face transforms with understanding. "Oh…"

"Quite a few people answered my question. Some gave joke responses, like *Psycho*. There were several that chose *Rear Window*, but after a few innocent questions, I eliminated them. But like I said, Kiera never made an appearance."

"It was a great idea."

"Apparently not as great as I thought it was."

I smile at him, so thankful for his support. My gaze lingers. Like a magnetic pull, I'm unable to look away until Zuri whines and her head pops up.

"Reid! Emerson!" It's Raina.

Reid grins. "We're upstairs!"

Zuri darts out of the room, and soon, we hear Raina's high-pitched terms of endearment for Zuri followed by unrhythmic thunder of their race up the stairs and down the hallway. Zuri reenters the room moments before a rosy-cheeked Raina makes an appearance.

"Hey." I slide off the bed to greet her. "How was your day?"

"Great!" As she peels off layers, she relays the details.

I sneak a peek at Reid. He glances my way, and we share a brief smile.

Raina tosses her scarf on top of the pile of outerwear that now covers the bed. "Mom said I could help you guys."

Reid hands her the tape measure. "Sounds good. We were just about to move on to the next room."

"Cool!" She skips out of the room ahead of us, with Zuri at her heels.

I take a few steps to follow them when Reid reaches out and touches my arm. I look into his dark eyes.

"Thanks for sharing all that." He keeps his voice low.

I nod.

"Hey!" Raina calls from the next room. "Are you guys coming?"

I smile. Her exuberance fills me with a mixture of sadness and joy as I'm reminded of my younger sisters.

Reid grins and rolls his eyes. "Yes, we're coming."

Chapter 16

We're just about finished eating the mouth-watering potpie Mrs. Stevenson brought over, when Dad breaks the amiable silence by tapping the table with his index finger.

"So," he says. "I was thinking, maybe I could pick up some Chinese tomorrow. You could choose the movie."

I stop swirling my fork through the sea of chicken and vegetables on my plate. "Yeah, sure. That sounds fine."

His gaze narrows in on me. "Do you not know what tomorrow is?"

"Friday?" And the start of yet another long weekend.

He grins. "It's Valentine's Day."

Oh. "No, I didn't think about it." Losing track of time has been a consequence of having few interactions with the outside world. Chinese food and watching some romantic comedy on Valentine's Day has been our family tradition for years. While I'm not sure how fun it will be with just the two of us, I can't say no. Dad's effort is so sweet. "Sounds good. How about *The Princess Bride?*"

"*Inconceivable!*"

I laugh at his impression of a favorite line, and then ponder whether that movie is the wisest choice. As a family, we had so much fun watching it over the years and blurting out the movie lines.

His eyes soften as he seems to read my mind. "Em, I know I've said this before, but I'm not sure you ever truly believe it. What happened is not your fault. There are bad people out there, and because of you, someday they will be behind bars where they can't hurt any more innocent people." He reaches over and squeezes my hand. "Maybe you were not in the wrong place at the wrong time. Maybe God put you in that very place at that exact moment for a reason."

He pushes away from the table and carries our plates to the sink, leaving his words to linger in the air. I'd never considered the possibility that God was using me and Keira to help others. And who did we really help? We couldn't save the Carters, and our families were hurt when we came forward with what we knew.

For the first time, I think about Reid's prayer, thanking God for protecting us. We'd crossed paths with some dangerous people, but as far as I know, we are all safe.

That is something to be thankful for.

~

The next afternoon, I'm curled up by the fireplace in our cabin, reading a book. Dad won't be home with our Chinese food for a while yet.

I turn the last page and suddenly regret devouring the book so fast. I've always been a bookworm, but something about reading the old books from the lodge library fills me with nostalgia—a longing for simpler times when people went calling on their neighbors on Sunday afternoons and didn't have to worry about corrupt politicians and lawmen. Then again, maybe the past wasn't as sweet as I'd like to believe. If it had been, why would the O'Malleys have felt the need to build hidden rooms and tunnels?

A knock on the front door and Zuri's barking pulls me back to the present with a sudden jolt of fear that it might be some marshal coming to tell us it's time to move again. I lean back in my chair. *Where did that thought come from?* I hadn't had those fears in weeks. Likely, an unforeseen consequence of dredging up the past.

Zuri's whining and leaping routine pushes away any doubt as she tells me in no uncertain terms who is on the front porch. I glance in the mirror hanging near the front door to ensure I look all right before greeting Reid.

I pull open the door to find him standing there, both hands behind his back. He hasn't said a word, but curiously, Zuri takes one look at him and sits at my feet, her ears perked and her tail wagging back and forth along the floor.

I look from Zuri to Reid. "Wow. Have you been taking my dog to obedience training behind my back? You need to share those magic powers with me."

He grins. "Sure." His left hand emerges from behind his back to reveal an enormous rawhide bone braided into the shape of a heart.

Zuri remains seated but lets out a pathetic whine, which makes us laugh.

"What else do you have hidden there?" I ask. "A raw steak?"

He shakes his head. "Nope." He brings a bouquet of roses into view.

"Oh!" Involuntarily, my hands cover my mouth. "Oh, my goodness. Are these for me?" I've never received flowers from a guy before. Even my homecoming date last fall neglected the tradition.

Reid hands Zuri her present and offers the bouquet to me. "I didn't think Zuri would appreciate flowers."

I step aside so he can enter the cabin and pull the flowers close to inhale their scent. "These smell amazing, and they're so pretty. Thank you." My face heats up with a blush. "I wasn't expecting this."

He stuffs his hands in the front pockets of his jeans. "I hope you don't mind. I just thought this Valentine's Day might be tough for you. If your mom is at all like mine, she probably made it a special day for the family."

"That's so thoughtful." I take a step forward in order to hug him, then change my mind and pivot toward the kitchen, too unsure of myself to follow through. "I should probably put these in water."

Reid follows me into the kitchen as Zuri plops on the floor, aggressively chomping on her new bone. That should keep her busy for some time. I begin a search through the cabinets for a vase. After three unsuccessful tries, Reid opens the cabinet above the fridge, grabs a vase, and hands it to me.

"Thanks." I begin fumbling with the plastic that's protecting the delicate flowers.

Reid leans against the counter beside me. "I figured Mom probably stocked this kitchen the same way she did ours." He watches me snip off the ends of the stems before speaking again. "I thought you might want to hang out for a while."

I glance at him as the vase fills with water. "You mean, right now?"

"Unless you have a better offer." His smile is warm and endearing.

"Oh. Um...well."

A shadow flits across his face and he looks away, but I see the telltale hitch of his Adam's apple. I've let him down.

I answer quickly. "I mean, I do have plans this evening...with my dad."

A sly grin crosses his face. "Actually, I think Raina cornered him this morning and asked if you guys would come to our house for dinner and a movie. From what I hear, he put up a valiant fight but was no match for my sister's tough bargaining skills. Although, she did compromise a little. Apparently, we are now having Chinese food and watching *The Princess Bride*. I was tasked with making sure you arrive at our home at precisely six o'clock, which means we have plenty of time to practice your skating before the evening's festivities."

I laugh as I arrange my flowers in the vase. "Well, I guess I'm the last to know. But that sounds like a fantastic plan." Satisfied with my work, I set the vase in the center of the kitchen table. "I'll get ready."

I've already turned and am headed to my room when he answers. "Great, then it's a date."

My heart leaps into my throat, and I wonder if he caught the brief hesitation in my step at his choice of words.

~

Zuri is so content with her bone that she doesn't even seem to mind when we leave her behind. As we enter the dining room of the lodge, I realize this was no impromptu idea. The twinkling

Christmas lights leading from the back porch to the frozen lake and the fire in the firepit add a magical glow to the late afternoon dimness. A sweet '50s tune plays from a speaker near the gazebo. I toss an appreciative smile Reid's way as we sit on the bench and put on our skates.

"This is all pretty amazing."

He shrugs. "Don't give me too much credit. I just recycled the party decorations."

"Well, it's absolutely perfect."

This time, I step on the ice with a little more confidence. Reid reaches for my hand just as the Beatles begin singing about wanting to hold hands. I smile at the perfect timing. Tonight, with heavy clouds blocking the night sky, the only twinkling is provided by the strands of lights. After a few strides, Reid twirls me. The uncoordinated move causes a collision, which makes me giggle. Soon, we're gliding in sync as the playlist switches to a classic Frank Sinatra song.

"Have you been practicing while I'm at school?" Reid asks. "You're doing great."

"I had a stellar teacher."

Hand in hand, we glide around the frozen lake. When I hit a rough patch in the ice, he grabs me with his free hand and keeps me from falling. We share a smile. When our gazes lock, everything else around us seems to disappear. All that exists is his handsome face and those caring eyes of his. Time seems to slow as we're lost in the moment, but we slowly come out of our trance when snowflakes drift down and land on us. One lands on Reid's long eyelashes, and I feel a cold speck on my nose. He dabs it with his glove, and we both laugh.

Soon, we're skating again, the enjoyment of the activity pushing away any thoughts of the cold—until I nearly go down again, this time due to the lack of feeling in my feet. Time to succumb to the reality of the situation before I injure myself. "Can we take a little break at the firepit to warm up?"

"Absolutely."

The ice skates and my numb feet slow our walk through the snow, but soon, we're sitting together on one of the benches in front of the fire Reid lit before coming to get me. I warm my hands as he places a blanket across my lap.

"Wow, you've really thought of everything."

His eyebrows wiggle as he reaches down and holds up a bright red thermos. "Even brought the cocoa."

"You are spoiling me, Mr. Stevenson."

"You deserve it."

I'm not sure I've done anything to deserve the attention of such a great guy…but I'm certainly not complaining. I watch him pour the steaming beverage, and silently vow to appreciate this relationship for as long as it lasts.

"Here you are, my lady." Reid smiles and hands me one of the cups.

I sip my drink and watch the dancing flames in front of us, happy for the chance to be living in the moment.

"Hey," Reid begins. Something about his tone makes me look at him. His face glows from the reflection of the fire. "I have to confess something."

"The cocoa's not homemade?" I tease.

His smile doesn't quite reach his eyes. *Uh, oh.* I brace myself for what's coming. Shoulda known this moment was too good to be true.

He sets down his mug and clasps his hands between his knees. "The thing is, I couldn't get your plan of reaching out to your cousin out of my mind."

Unease slithers up my spine. "What did you do?"

He holds my gaze. "I went on the site you told me about."

Panic and anger surge through me. "Reid! How could you? You might have put us in danger."

He raises a hand. "Hear me out. I scrolled through the past messages and found your post from several months ago. I searched all of the responses, especially the newer ones."

Curiosity squelches my rising fear. "And?"

"There were a few more *Rear Window* answers, and it got me wondering. What if there was a different movie title that Keira responded with?"

"I doubt it. *Rear Window* is so fitting."

"What about *39 Steps*? It was a movie that only one person responded with. Since I'm unfamiliar with Hitchcock's films, I did a little research, and I think the storyline might fit the situation."

I shake my head but then begin to remember the movie's plot. It isn't one of my favorites, but the premise begins to come to me. The main character keeps having to change his identity as he tries to figure out a crime. Reid is right—it could fit. Would Keira have responded with that answer? It would be just like her to find a more obscure film to respond with. How did I not think of it?

Reid is intently watching me. "Well?"

"Yeah, that might've been her." A mixture of excitement and anxiety fills me. This might be the break I've been looking for. But could pursuing it cause more problems? I certainly don't want to relocate again. Too overwhelmed to think clearly, I take a sip of my cocoa.

His face clouds with obvious concern. "Are you okay?"

"I'm not sure."

"Well, what was the next part of your plan if you found someone you thought could be Keira? Do you have a message to respond with?"

I let out a breath. "Reid, what if this triggers something bad, and Dad and I have to move again?"

"I thought about that, and honestly, it would be devastating." Our eyes lock as unspoken thoughts simmer between us. He shifts positions. "But forget about my feelings. This is about you. It's your decision. We can let it go, or we can send a message and see if there's a response."

I close my eyes, unsure of what to do. The risks are so high.

"For what it's worth, I think you should respond and see what happens." His voice is calm and soothing. "It might haunt you if you don't."

Then again, it might haunt me if I *do*. But he's probably right. I hesitantly nod and open my eyes.

He removes his gloves and pulls his phone from his coat pocket. "Okay, what do you want to ask?"

I'd had plenty of time to think about this when I first came up with the idea. I answer without hesitation. "*What is the key to solving the mystery?*"

Reid studies my face for final approval.

I nod.

He pulls up the website and types in my question. When he's finished, he returns the phone to his pocket and pulls the gloves up over his hands. "Now we'll just wait and see what happens. In the meantime, we'd better get going. I don't want to face Raina's wrath if we're late."

"We certainly don't want that. Do you think we have time for me to change?" A dinner-and-a-movie night calls for comfy clothes.

"Sure. We have to stop there anyway because I'm under strict orders to deliver both you and Zuri."

I laugh. "Excellent. Sounds like the perfect evening."

He offers his hand, and I place mine in it. As we gingerly wobble our way toward our boots, I wonder what the rest of my family is doing tonight. *Please, God, let them know how much I love them.*

Chapter 17

The sound of the back door clicking shut wakes me. Snuggling deeper within my cozy bed, I hear the rumble of Dad's truck and the eventual crunching of snow beneath the tires. It takes a moment for my mind to fully engage. It's Saturday morning. Dad and Mr. Stevenson are driving to the Twin Cities to gather supplies. Dad invited me along, offering once again to drop me off for a day of shopping at the Mall of America. But I politely declined due to the early departure time. One of these days, I'll go with him.

I roll over, anticipating another hour or so of sleep, and come face-to-face with Zuri. Her pink tongue, with the unique black splotches in the center, darts out and licks my nose. Ugh. I roll back the other way, but then I feel her paw tap my back. Over and over. And over. So much for sleeping in.

I push away the covers and glare at my dog. At the moment, she's not as cute as she thinks she is. "I was trying to sleep, ya know."

She answers with a high-pitched yowl.

"You're not fooling me. Dad always feeds you and lets you out before he leaves."

Her head tilts as she watches my slow movements.

"Fine." I pull on a comfy, oversized sweatshirt and head to the kitchen. The first thing I see are the beautiful flowers from Reid.

I sink down in a chair and touch the delicate petals. I noticed Dad's slight frown as he glanced at the bouquet last night when we returned from the movie, but thankfully, he said nothing. "Oh, Zur. What are we going to do? I think I'm falling for him."

Her tail thumps against the wood floor.

"You, too?"

She barks.

"Why is life so complicated?" I peer out the window at the gently falling snow. The fluffy white flakes twist and twirl as they dance through the sky.

Zuri has always had an uncanny ability to recognize my inner turmoil. She offers comfort by rubbing against my legs. The black hairs she leaves behind match my leggings.

"What do you think, girl? Is it possible that Keira sent that message?"

She rests her head on my lap, her brown eyes peering up at me.

"You're right. Worrying about it won't change anything. So what should we do today?"

She lifts her head, ears perked.

I stroke her silky head. "Without a vehicle, our options are pretty limited. I guess a walk and searching for a new book to read are on the agenda." Her backend shimmies as she wags her tail. "I know what you're thinking. We should check on Reid and Raina to see what they're doing today. But we don't want them to think we're too needy and pathetic."

Of course, if they could see me now, having a conversation with my dog, that is precisely what they would be thinking.

An hour later, I'm perusing the bookshelves at the lodge library. The choices have been narrowed down to *Gone with the Wind*, *Frankenstein*, and *Murder on the Orient Express*.

I'm thumbing through the pages when my phone rings. Mrs. Grier's name shows on the screen.

I set down the book to answer. "Hello?"

"Good morning, Emerson. Are you enjoying this snowy Saturday?"

"Yes, I am. I'm actually searching for my next book to read."

"What a perfect day for that." She clears her throat. "I've been thinking a lot about your quest to discover more about the O'Malleys, and I may have a new path for you to pursue."

"Really?"

"Yes. I kept wracking my brain to remember if there were any O'Malley relatives left in the area, but I couldn't think of any. Then I remembered that James O'Malley's wife, Margaret, also grew up here. I did a little digging and found that she has a niece, Madeline Benson, who still lives in Minnesota, at a retirement home in Austin."

My interest took a sudden leap. Maybe Ms. Benson could fill in some pieces to the puzzle. "Do you think she would talk to me?"

"I know she would. I just spoke with her myself. She said she would be happy to talk with you on the phone." Mrs. Grier pauses for just a moment. "But what she would really love would be a visit. Is there any way you could drive down and see her one of these days?"

"Yes, that would definitely work." Once I find a day when Dad doesn't need the truck, and then somehow convince him to let me drive to Austin. My hopes sag, knowing that would be a nearly impossible feat. He always seems reluctant to even let me drive the truck into nearby Hermann.

"Wonderful. I'll text you her information."

"Thank you so much, Mrs. Grier."

"Glad I could help. I've always been fascinated by that family's history as well, so I'll be interested in what she has to tell you. I sure hope you find some answers."

"I do, too."

After hanging up, I immediately call Reid to share the news, completely forgetting my resolve of not bothering him today.

"Austin, huh?" he says, after I relay the message.

"Yeah. I'm thinking I can probably drive down one day this week. Is it very far?"

"Nah, it's about an hour away." He's quiet for a few moments. "Hey, why don't we go today?"

My heart skips a beat. "I wasn't trying to coerce a ride from you."

"I know. But it'll be fun. There's a lot to see in Austin."

"Well, if you're sure." Interviewing an O'Malley relative while spending the afternoon with Reid—what could be better?

"Absolutely."

"Okay, let me call my dad and let him know."

I have to use a bit of persuasion, but Dad eventually agrees on one condition: Reid and I need to stop by a store for him and Mr. Stevenson, saving them a trip. As a bonus, I won't have to feel guilty about leaving Zuri since Raina insists that the two of them need an afternoon together, perfecting the tricks they've been working on.

Soon, we're on our way. Reid's eclectic playlist consists of alternative rock and modern country. I lean back and watch light flakes of snow drift from the gray sky as we cruise down the road.

Our first stop is the lighting store that Dad added to our itinerary. We pick up a crate of lamps that Mrs. Stevenson ordered for the guest rooms. Errand finished, we continue our southbound journey.

"Next stop, Austin?" I glance at my handsome driver.

"Not yet. First, we need to swing by Clarks Grove."

I frown in confusion. "Is that a town, or somebody's orchard?"

He grins. "It's a town with a very unique statue. My grandpa took me there once when he was visiting, and I've wanted to go back ever since."

"Speaking of grandpas..." Honestly, I didn't want to pester him about the Hitchcock message board, but the segue was too perfect to pass up. "Did you happen to check for a reply from our *39 Steps* friend?"

He nods, seeming unfazed by my clunky change of subject. "I checked this morning, but there wasn't anything yet. I *did* add a notification alert so we won't miss it when they do respond."

"Thanks."

He glances at me and smiles. "Sure thing." He returns his attention to the road. "I'm glad you and your dad joined us last night. It's been a while since I've seen that movie. I forgot how good it was."

"Just a few more viewings, and you, too, can blurt out the lines."

"I doubt I'll ever be as good as you."

"Obviously not," I tease.

We continue the drive, with easy conversation about favorite movies, shows, vacations, and memories. Getting to be myself and not worrying about giving away too much personal info in every little thing I say is an incredible gift—even better than those beautiful roses Reid gave me. On second thought, maybe it's not *that* great. I turn away to hide the blush my thoughts produce.

Time zips by at the same speed as the scenery that whizzes past in a blur. Soon, we're pulling off the highway and approaching a small town. A few turns later, we arrive at our destination.

I stare at the statue for a moment, then look at Reid. "You've been wanting to come back *here* for *years*?"

He nods, gazing at the object of his admiration.

"And for some reason," I continue, "you thought I would be the perfect person to also appreciate this masterpiece?"

He turns to look at me and grins. "Oh, yes. You see, since you're living in Minnesota, you need to appreciate the finer things the state has to offer."

"Like a giant fish?"

His eyebrows raise. "This is not just any giant fish. It is a bass."

"Oh!" I widen my eyes with mock admiration. "Well, in that case, I *am* impressed."

"I knew you would be. Picture time." He opens his door and steps out of the car.

I pull on my gloves, adjust my earmuffs, then leave the cocoon of warmth. We take numerous selfies with the ginormous leaping fish. A friendly passerby stops and offers to snap a few shots of us. At our cameraman's suggestion, we pose on either side of the fish, our arms wrapped around the enormous creature in a huge hug. At the last moment, Reid reaches out a little further and grasps my hand.

Our amusement of Minnesota roadside attractions continues as we drive to Austin. We stop to admire a giant fork sticking out of the ground, a massive cow named Buffy, and a kid's-sized chapel.

"I had no idea Minnesota had so much to offer." I slide back into Reid's SUV after our last stop.

"Oh, there is much more to show you." He starts the car. "Ready for lunch?"

"Yes, I'm starving. What do you have in mind?" There must be a cute little diner around here where we can eat before our two o'clock appointment with Margaret's niece.

"We're having SPAM."

"SPAM?"

He nods. "Yes, ma'am. You can't come to Austin, Minnesota, the SPAM capital of the world, and not enjoy the local delicacy of canned meat."

I study his face. "Are you serious?"

"Yep. And you're in for a treat. The deli at the SPAM museum offers all kinds of unique concoctions."

I buckle my seatbelt. "Well, you haven't steered me wrong yet. What's the saying? When in Austin…?"

"That's the spirit!"

I can't say that SPAM is my favorite food. In fact, I'm not sure I ever need to consume it again. But I have to admit that the Monte Python Café is the most unique dining venue I've ever visited. The museum provides the backdrop for more fun selfies as we peruse the various displays of SPAM history, ads, and vintage commercials. Who knew canned meat was such a cultural phenomenon?

Reid plops a paper hat on my head and leads me to a seven-step mock assembly line. "Ready to see if you've got what it takes to produce a can of SPAM?"

"Absolutely."

I try my hand at the various stages of production, but I'm unable to control my giggles. Reid's paper hat keeps slipping over his eyes while he's concentrating on labeling one of the rectangular-shaped cans. Despite his fumbling, he finally achieves his goal, while I can barely see the can in front of me through my tears of laughter.

"Emerson," he scolds, "you are not taking this job seriously."

I wipe my eyes. "Sorry. I guess being SPAM Employee of the Month is not in my future."

"Maybe this will be more up your alley." He pulls off his paper hat and directs me toward a computer screen with an interactive game.

Following the instructions, we take turns virtually launching a fork with a catapult. Suddenly, our visit to the giant fork in the ground makes a bit more sense.

My cartoon fork soars past Reid's. "Take that!" I yell.

He groans.

As with any good trip to a museum, our visit ends in the gift shop, where we are unable to resist the trinkets.

With purchases in hand, we stroll toward the exit. Always the gentleman, Reid holds the door for me. "I still can't believe you wouldn't try the pumpkin spice SPAM."

I shiver in disgust. "At least we have matching souvenirs." I pull out my mini knight keychain.

"How have we lived this long without a Sir Can-a-lot?"

"We really have been missing out." I put my new purchase in my pocket and pull my coat tighter around me. "I'm still not as convinced as you are that Raina will appreciate the bacon SPAM you bought her."

He grins. "Well, if she doesn't like it, I'm sure Zuri will. I still think Margaret's niece would have enjoyed a can."

I shake my head. "Nope. I'm sticking with my veto on that idea. The gift shop lady told me about a candy shop not far from here. I think a nice box of chocolates will be a more welcomed gift."

"If you insist." He shrugs.

Twenty minutes later, we're checked in at the retirement home and knocking on Madeline Benson's door.

"Come in." The voice is soft and wispy.

Inside, an older woman sits in a large chair. I'm not sure if the chair is oversized or if she's just tiny, but the piece of furniture seems to envelope her. Her white hair is pulled into a bun, while the thick lenses of her glasses magnify pale-blue eyes.

"Hi, Mrs. Benson." I hold out my right hand.

A thin, bony arm reaches out from her loose-fitting peach cardigan. I take her hand in a gentle grasp, afraid I might damage her if I squeeze too hard.

"Please, call me Madeline." When she smiles, I glimpse the vibrant woman she probably once was.

"It's so nice to meet you. I'm Emerson, and this is Reid."

He gently shakes her hand, then takes a seat on a nearby sofa that matches Mrs. Benson's chair.

"These are for you for taking the time to chat with us." I hand her the box of candy, and then take a seat beside Reid.

She studies the pretty box with a smile. "How did you know my weakness? Thank you."

I nudge Reid and give him an I-told-you-so smile.

Madeline sets the box on the table next to her, between a glass of water and a box of tissues. "Mrs. Grier said you were researching Aunt Maggie and Uncle Jimmy."

Hearing Margaret and James' nicknames adds a new, personal dimension. These were not just historical names, they were real people that this woman had loved.

Reid nods. "My family bought the O'Malley lodge, and Emerson and I have become interested in its history."

"There are so many unusual stories about the place and the family. We would love to uncover the truth," I add.

She sighs. "Yes. That poor family. Some say the O'Malleys were cursed. They certainly faced a lot of tragedy." Leaning back, she disappears further into her chair. "From what I understand, the first two generations of O'Malleys were devoutly religious. However, that seemed to change when James O'Malley III faced financial ruin during the Great Depression. It seems that particular James lost his faith. It's hard to blame him for searching for ways to keep the lodge open and running during those desperate times, but he turned the place into a speakeasy."

She glances at us. "In case you don't know what a speakeasy is, it was an establishment that illegally sold alcohol during Prohibition. That is really when the family's good fortune took a turn for the worse." The tiny woman's head moves side to side, sadness turning her blue eyes a misty gray. "Wealthy folks from Chicago and Minneapolis flooded to the lake to enjoy alcohol and gambling during Prohibition. Most people in the area had suspicions about what was happening, but for better or worse, they kept quiet."

"I read there was a death on the property during that time." I coax gently when she goes quiet, lost in thought.

She draws a deep breath and clasps small, wrinkled hands in her lap. "Oh, yes. A young woman drowned. The shocking death brought with it scandalous stories of dapper men and girls in their flapper dresses, dancing, drinking, and carrying on at all hours of the night. After that, the O'Malley name took a huge hit. They were ostracized." She releases a heavy sigh. "After Prohibition ended, the lodge continued to be a destination for big city folks. Some claimed that Chicago mobsters began to frequent the place. I don't know about that, but eventually, the city visitors found new travel destinations. Anyway, local families held a grudge and refused to return to the lodge. I believe hunters stayed there in the fall, but otherwise, it sat empty."

Reid's phone buzzes. He glances at it, then mouths, "Mom."

I nod before turning back to Madeline. "Can you tell us about your Aunt Margaret and the youngest James O'Malley?"

"My mother spoke about them quite often. At first, our family worried about their relationship, since the O'Malley name was poorly thought of. But they eventually grew to love Jimmy. He was a good man and treated Margaret like a princess. The two of them were determined to bring back honor to his family name."

Both Reid and I sense there was more to the story, so we remain quiet.

Madeline continues without any urging from us. "When Pearl Harbor was attacked, Uncle Jimmy enlisted in the military. Everyone was so proud of him. My mother told me that his unit was involved in liberating one of the concentration camps. He never talked about what he experienced, but it seemed to change him. His main priority became renovating the lodge, even though the demons of war seemed to haunt him."

I shiver. *Geez. Who wouldn't be traumatized by that experience?* "We heard that your Aunt Margaret died fairly young."

Even after all these years, the pain in her eyes is evident. "Oh, that was so sad. Aunt Maggie and their young son, James O'Malley VI, both died in a car accident. She lost control on an icy bridge, and they plunged into a ravine."

Reid's phone buzzes again. After glancing down at it, he looks at me. "Sorry. Raina."

I offer a smile, and then turn my attention back to Madeline. "That's horrible." While certainly tragic, I'm oddly relieved their deaths came about by accident. I hadn't liked the rumors of foul play.

"Did your family keep in touch with James after Margaret's death?" Reid asks.

Her forehead creases, adding new lines to her wrinkled face. "My mother tried. But Uncle Jimmy was so distraught. He lost interest in just about everything, including fixing up the lodge. Soon, he was a recluse. We heard rumors that he lived in the woods, but we weren't sure he was even still in the area. That is, until we heard of his death."

I reach out and place my hand on one of hers. "What a tragic story."

She pats the back of my hand with her free one. "It is quite sad, but I've always believed it's a good example of what can become of your life if you don't have a relationship with God. Several of the O'Malley men turned away from their faith. I often wonder how different things might have been if they had kept their hands in His."

Madeline holds my gaze for a few moments, as if her message is meant specifically for me. Ridiculous. She couldn't possibly know about my own struggles with faith.

I smile and lean back in my seat. "Well, thank you for answering our questions and spending so much time with us."

We stay a few more minutes chatting, and then make our exit.

On the way to the car, I'm still pondering Madeline's message when Reid's phone buzzes for the third time.

"You're certainly popular today. Everything okay at home?" Hopefully, Zuri is behaving herself.

He scans his phone, then looks at me. "The first message was from my mom. She invited you and your dad for dinner again. We're having homemade pizzas. The second message was Raina, chiming in to tell me you can't decline Mom's offer because she and Zuri have been working hard all afternoon on some tricks that everyone must see tonight."

Who knew that dog could get even more spoiled?

He opens the passenger car door for me, and I slide inside the cold car.

Reid settles in behind the wheel, starts the car, and then turns to look at me.

"What?" I ask, trying to read his expression.

"The last message was a notification that our *39 Steps* friend responded."

I suck in a breath. "Oh. Wow. What did they say?"

He holds up his phone. "Ready to find out?"

I'm barely breathing as I nod. *Keira, have I actually found you?*

He pulls up the message and holds the phone between us. I lean close as we read the message: *Her sleight of hand is the key.*

He watches me as I reread the message. "Well? Does it mean anything to you?"

I bite my lower lip as I try to remember the movie, wishing I'd seen it more than once. The two main characters end up hand-cuffed together. The situation causes some entertaining scenes, until the female lead manages to slip her hand out of the cuffs, freeing them. While it's an intriguing message, I see no correlation to our situation, it's just emphasizing the plot.

My shoulders sag with disappointment. "I don't think that's her."

The pity etched on his face is almost too much to handle. "I'm sorry."

"It's okay. I should have known not to get my hopes up."

"I'll keep checking the site. Maybe something else will pop up."

"Maybe." *Or maybe it's time to let it go.*

As Reid pulls out of the parking lot, I change the subject to Madeline and all that she revealed. "That was nice of Mrs. Benson to tell us so much."

"It definitely filled in some holes." Reid keeps his eyes on the road.

"I'm glad James didn't kill his wife, but it was still such a heart-breaking end to her life."

"I know." Reid shakes his head. "Still, how sad that he was never able to honor the family name again."

"He actually discredited it even more. And we still don't know what the hidden space in the second bedroom was created for."

"So much for solving our mystery." He glances over his shoulder and merges into traffic.

I spend the rest of the drive scanning all the goofy photos we took. There are so many funny ones to commemorate our day, but my favorite by far is of us holding hands as we hugged that ridiculous giant bass. Who knows what the future holds, but at least I'll always have these pictures to remember my wonderful day with this special guy.

~

Later that night, Dad unlocks the front door of the cabin with only the dim porch light to illuminate the task. Zuri bounds in, still exuberant from an evening of performing her new repertoire of tricks—and the numerous treats she received for flawlessly executing every one of them.

I hang my coat on the hook by the door. "Think we can get Zur to jump through a hoop too, or is Raina the only one with the magic charm?"

Dad slips out of his jacket. "If you give her enough treats, I'm sure she'll oblige. I especially liked the army crawl, rolling over, and playing dead routine."

"Who knew we had such a ham?" I pat Zuri's head.

"Want a glass of water before bed?" Dad asks as he strides toward the kitchen.

"Sure, thanks."

He flips on the light, revealing the beautiful Valentine's Day bouquet decorating the table. I glance at him, and he returns my gaze before turning toward the cupboard to the left of the sink. I've been waiting for him to say something about the gift—guess now is that moment.

He opens the cupboard door and pulls out two glasses. "Those are some pretty flowers. I'm guessing they're from Reid."

Assuming a snappy reply about them being from Cupid would not be appreciated, I simply answer, "Yep."

He fills the glasses with ice and water. "Reid seems like a nice guy, but our lives are rather complicated at the moment." He turns and hands me a glass.

Does he think I need reminding? "Dad, I know we might not be here for very long. It's just been nice having a friend to do things with and living a somewhat normal life. I promise I won't get too attached." I'm pretty sure it's already too late for that, but that's for the future me to worry about.

He leans in and kisses my forehead. "Okay, kid. Goodnight. See you in the morning for church."

"And brunch," I add.

He grins. "And brunch."

With one last lingering look at my gorgeous roses, I turn off the light and head to my room. Zuri leaps onto the bed and makes herself comfortable as I get ready. I slide beneath the covers, scooching bed-hog Zuri to her side of the bed, and then reach for my new read—*Gone with the Wind*. Lugging this massive hardcover copy around will not only keep me busy for a while, but it may prove to be a sufficient arm workout.

Arranging the pillows, I prop myself up and open the cover. A quick flip past the title page and the introduction, and I'm ready to be swept away by the romance of Scarlett and Rhett, but the words of Margaret Mitchell are not what I find.

Someone has painstakingly cut a rectangular hole in the pages. A small, leather journal is hidden within the covers of the book. *Whoa.*

I sit up to further examine my discovery. Carefully, I lift out the journal, which is tied shut with a thin strip of leather. With trembling fingers, I undo the knot and open the little book. Written in tight cursive, the words *The O'Malley Legacy,* are the first I see. *Oh, wow!* I turn the page, anxious to delve into the family's secrets, but the words are gibberish. The letters and numbers that are grouped together are nonsense—a code of some sort. *Interesting.*

I snap a few photos and send them off to Reid. *Looks like we have another mystery on our hands.*

After returning the journal to its hiding place, I put the novel on my bedside table. Then I nestle into my bed, anticipating dreams of coded messages and a wonderfully silly adventure with a handsome boy.

Chapter 18

"Good morning." The cute, elderly priest welcomes the congregation in his typical mumbling, subdued manner. "I hope you all had a wonderful time with your loved ones while celebrating St. Valentine's Day."

My insides warm as I remember the special moments I shared with Reid over the past few days.

"There are some interesting stories about Saint Valentine." The priest's gaze remains fixed on his sheet of paper.

Remembering Mrs. Grier's advice, I close my eyes so I'm not distracted by the man's lack of communication skills.

"We know very little about St. Valentine. He is most often associated with love, but we also know he was imprisoned and eventually martyred. I personally like the theory that he was jailed for secretly performing wedding ceremonies. We are used to hearing about saints who were martyred for their faith. But have you ever thought about the laypeople who followed their faith, like the couples that St. Valentine married? With Christian marriages being such a serious offense, why would couples take the risk to get married?" His papers rattle as he pauses for people to ponder his question.

Mrs. Grier was right—the priest's calm voice is quite soothing. Using her trick has diminished the dull, monotonous tone, and I'm able to concentrate on his words instead of his delivery.

"I think it's absolutely beautiful," he continues, "that those men and women knew what an incredibly important sacrament marriage is between a man and a woman. They could have kept their love and Christian beliefs hidden, but they knew how important it was to proclaim their faith. Ultimately, it didn't matter what others thought. They knew there was no hiding from God. How much more should we, who have no laws or restrictions on religion, boldly embrace and proclaim our faith?"

A lengthy pause follows. I sneak a peek at him taking a sip of water. His hands shake as he raises and lowers the cup. I squeeze my eyes shut again when it looks like he's ready to continue his homily.

"Are you trying to hide something from God?"

I shift in my seat, glad my eyes are closed so I can't see if he's directing his question at me...because it sure feels like he could be.

"Or perhaps you're keeping Him at the edge of your life. Well, as we near Lent, I want to challenge you all to seriously consider your relationship with God. Take some time to ponder your blessings and the responsibility entrusted to you to share your faith with others. I pray each of you will make the decision to go all in and give everything to the Lord.

As the Mass continues, his words reverberate in my brain. They remind me of what Reid said. Is it time to let go of my anger and blame so I can put God back in charge? Is that even possible? I didn't feel like my prayers were answered, but is it possible He's answering them in a different way?

After the service, I'm exiting the pew when I notice a familiar face. Mrs. Grier is at the back of the church, chatting with a group of ladies. Leaving Dad's side, I weave my way around the slow-moving congregants to reach her.

Her face brightens when she sees me, and she steps away from her friends to greet me. "Emerson! Good morning."

"Good morning. I wanted to thank you for the homily tip. I was actually able to pay attention today."

She smiles. "Glad to be of service. I've been so curious about your visit with Margaret's niece. How did it go?"

"It was great," I reply. "She was able to shed some light on a few details." Not to mention the amazing day I shared with Reid.

"Oh, that's wonderful. Why don't you shoot me an email when you get a chance and tell me all about it." She wiggles her fingers, mimicking typing on a keyboard.

"Will do." I smile at her, then turn to see Dad waiting for me by the front door, his expression puzzled. That's when it hits me—a vision of someone else doing the same motion as Mrs. Grier. Suddenly, the world has slowed to half speed, and I'm walking through sludge. *Am I experiencing déjà vu? Remembering a dream? Or is it a real memory? But from when?* My mind reels as I follow Dad to the car. *Where did I see that motion before? And why does it feel like it's important to remember?*

Dad doesn't seem to notice my preoccupation as he drives the short distance to Mabel's. Nor does he mention it when Mabel has to tell me twice that today's special is huevos rancheros. Instead, he calmly sips our hostess's delicious coffee.

I tap my fingernail against my mug of cocoa, unable to mellow my brewing internal turmoil. A few brain synapses finally connect, and I realize I need to run my thoughts by someone. My first instinct is to hurry through brunch and confide in Reid as soon as we get home. But then I look up at my dad, who seems to have finally noticed my distraction. He's watching me with concern in his eyes. This man, who has been my rock, is the person I need to talk to. *Hopefully, he won't freak.*

"Everything okay?" he finally asks.

Mabel walks past us, a large, noisy family following her. I take advantage of the increased decibel level and lean forward. "Dad, I think I remembered something."

"What?" The tone with which he delivers that one word makes it obvious he thinks I'm talking about something as mundane as forgetting to give Zuri clean water or taking out the trash.

I hold his gaze until something shifts on his face, and I know he fully understands.

He leans closer. "You mean, from *that* night?"

I nod. "At least, I think it's a real memory. Something Mrs. Grier did at church triggered it."

His eyes narrow. "Go on."

"That night, when we were peering in the Clarks' window, and Mrs. Clark suddenly turned and seemed to look at us, Keira and I froze for a moment. Then we convinced ourselves that because of the dark night and the bright room, it was impossible for her to see us. We laughed at our paranoid reaction and left. But there's a little detail that just popped into my mind. I think she was doing something with her hands."

His brows furrow in confusion.

"I'm pretty sure she started moving her fingers as she was staring out the window." I mimic typing to show him what I mean. The simple movement suddenly sends a jolt of realization through me. *A sleight of hand.* That's what our *39 Steps* friend wrote—*her sleight of hand is the key. Whoa.* Maybe that message was from Keira, and she remembered the same thing. Ideas begin to percolate.

I lean forward and my hair slides over my shoulder to cascade onto the table. "Do you think Mrs. Clark could have been trying to convey a message? Maybe she *did* see us, but we didn't understand what she was trying to tell us." My eyes fill with tears. "And we ignored it."

He reaches out and squeezes my hand. "Em, don't do this to yourself."

"But Dad," I whisper. "The more I think about it, the more sure I am that she was sending a message. But we didn't pay attention, and now she's dead."

He's quiet for a moment before responding. "If she was trying to signal for assistance, wouldn't she have tried to mouth the word *help*? Or pretend she was talking on her phone or texting? Mimicking typing doesn't really invoke a sense of urgency."

"Yeah, I guess. But what else could she have been doing?"

"Maybe it was a nervous habit."

My eyes widen as a new idea forms. "Or maybe she was sending a clue."

"About what?"

"What if she knew something about the D.A. and was trying to tell us about some incriminating information on one of their computers?"

He looks far from convinced. "Em, I'm sure all of their computers were thoroughly searched. Anything remotely important would have been found."

His protest fails to dampen my new conviction. "Dad, we've always assumed that some of the police officers were compromised. Seems to me there are two possibilities. Either they searched the computers and destroyed the evidence they found, or they never bothered to look since the deaths were ruled an accident."

My argument must possess some logic because he doesn't dismiss my hypothesis. So I continue to press the point. "You yourself recently said maybe God put us there for a specific reason." Something sparks in my mind. "It's like Esther in the Bible, maybe I was born for a time such as this and am the one who is meant to figure it out."

Weariness descends upon him. "How sure are you that it's what really happened, and not just something your imagination conjured up?"

I contemplate his excellent question, wishing I had an equally worthy answer. "I'm not sure at all. I suppose it might not have happened, but I can picture it so clearly. I'm pretty sure it's a real memory. After we found out about the Clarks' deaths, I was so shocked that I tried not to think about what we'd seen. And later, we were focused on the men they were meeting with that the other details were forgotten."

He slowly nods, but the corners of his mouth turn down.

"Do you think we should tell the marshal?" I press. Maybe my memory means nothing, but what if it's important?

He strokes the side of his face. "I'll let him know. But you need to keep in mind that this probably won't lead to anything. I don't want you getting your hopes up."

I let out a sigh of relief. "I won't. Thanks for believing me."

His smile doesn't quite reach his eyes. "I'll always believe you."

Chapter 19

Sunday afternoon finds me in the lodge's library with Reid. He examines the small, leather journal I found inside *Gone with the Wind* as I finish telling him about my memory.

"Geez, I can't leave you alone for a minute," he jokes. "But seriously, it's amazing you remembered that detail. So it probably was Kiera we were communicating with."

I shrug. "Maybe. Although, I'm not even sure it is a true memory. Even if it's accurate, what are the chances Mrs. Clark was actually trying to send a message? And if she was trying to tell us there's incriminating evidence on her computer about the D.A., will the police ever discover it? As much as I'd like to figure this out, there's nothing I can do about it now." I point toward the journal. "That's why I'm ready for a distraction. Want to help me decipher a message?"

He nods. "Let's do it."

We open the journal and stare at the jumble of words.

"Well, assuming the single letters are *a's and i's*, maybe we can figure out some of the words and determine the cipher," Reid suggests.

"Excellent."

However, after twenty minutes, we realize the plan is not quite as excellent as I hoped.

Reid pulls out his phone. "Let me search for different ciphers and codes."

After we try each and every suggestion, I lean against the couch, frustration eroding my optimism. "Maybe he left a key to the code in one of the secret rooms?"

"It's worth a look." Reid stands and reaches for my hand, then pulls me to my feet.

However, a complete and thorough search of the lodge yields nothing.

Back in the library, I pace in front of the fireplace. "What are we missing?"

Reid sinks back into the velvety sofa. "Hey, what about those books that were in the pool room?"

Why hadn't I thought of that? Maybe they were set aside for a reason. I turn toward the shelf where the books are now resting and grab the stack in question. Then I join Reid on the couch, placing the books between us. We diligently page through each book, but ultimately come up empty.

I let out a heavy breath, then stare at the shelves. *We're missing something. What is it?*

"Do we start looking through each book?" Reid asks.

I groan. There must be a hundred books here. As I scan the symmetrical shelves, I wonder who so perfectly synchronized them. The lodge had different owners over the years, so it most likely wasn't James or Margaret who arranged all of the items. So, why should the code still be here? Then again, maybe one of the O'Malleys *did* place the items on the shelves. One of the articles Mrs. Grier had given me stated that the rehab facility had tried to leave things exactly as they were to preserve the lodge's history.

I stare at the shelves. Why were the O'Malleys so meticulous in their decorating? An idea sparks. James' journal was hidden on the right side of the fireplace, inside a book. Could the cipher reside in the same spot on the left side? My gaze travels to the empty spot on the right-side shelf, where *Gone with the Wind* was nestled next to an ornate bookend. I zero in on the left side and the nearly mirror image of a large carved bookend and a fat book beside it. I quickly get to my feet.

"You figured something out, didn't you?"

"Doubtful, but it's worth checking."

I stride to the bookshelf on the left of the fireplace and retrieve the book in the same spot that coincided with *Gone with the Wind's* location on the right. With *Moby Dick* clutched in my hands, I return to the couch and have a seat beside Reid.

Slowly, we page through the book. All seems normal until we get to page 101. The page number is circled. We scan the page, and Reid's finger lands on a letter in the middle of the page that is also circled. We turn and look at each other, excitement sizzling between us.

The next twenty-five pages have their page numbers circled, as well as a random letter. The ten pages following them have a number that is circled.

"Okay," I say, "let's assume for the moment that page 101's letter corresponds with the letter *a*, and so forth."

"Makes sense," Reid agrees.

We begin matching the miscellaneous letters to the letters of the alphabet. I call out letters, while Reid jots them down next to the corresponding letter in the alphabet. Then we do the same with the numbers. With that chore behind us, we painstakingly unravel the message.

> *My great-great-grandaddy James O' Malley I - born 1825 Tipperary Ireland - moved to America when he was a child. In 1850, he homesteaded our family land, where he built a small cabin at the edge of the lake.*

I look up at Reid. "Those dates match with what I discovered at the library."

"Think this is the spot of the first cabin?" Reid asks.

I shrug and turn to the next entry.

> *My great-grandaddy, James O'Malley II, was born in 1850 here in the great state of Minnesota. I heard stories of how he and his father built a shack with a hidden cellar on the land, for use as an Underground Railroad stop.*

A shiver courses down my spine. *Oh, wow.*

Reid's eyes light up. "That old shack once sheltered runaway slaves."

I'm filled with an odd sense of relief. "I've become so attached to this place and the O'Malley family, it makes me happy to know they were good people."

"At least, some of them were," he points out.

We continue our discovery.

My grandpa, James O'Malley III, was born in 1875 here in Minnesota. He began construction on the lodge in 1912, offering a place to stay for city folk who liked to come to the Minnesota lakes during the summer.

My father, James O'Malley IV, was born in 1900 here in Minnesota. My father often spoke about the struggles of WWI and the stock market crash. Because times were tough, he convinced his father to turn the lodge into a speakeasy. Grandpa refused for a while. He agreed only after things became desperate. My father added a secret room with a bar and a pool table. He even put in access stairs from his upstairs bedroom. In order to smuggle in the booze, he built a tunnel connecting the lodge and the old cabin.

When the townsfolk discovered what my family was doing, we lost all respectability. My mother was devastated, and my father began to drink too much. Eventually, the out-of-towners found new places to go. The O'Malley name was ruined, and the lodge sat empty.

All of that matched with what we'd learned from Margaret's niece.

I am James O'Malley V – born in 1925 here in Minnesota. I grew up with a disgraced father and a grandfather who wished for a way to restore the family name. That desire was passed on to me. I married my beautiful bride, Margaret, who shares my dream of bringing respect back to the O'Malley family.

After the attack on Pearl Harbor, I enlisted to fight in WWII. I wanted to defend our great country from the Nazis, but I also hoped to bring honor to the O'Malley name.

I am home now from the war. Margaret says I'm a changed man. But how do you return to normal after seeing the face of evil? We wiped out the Nazis, but wickedness has a way of resurfacing. After all, evil had not been completely eliminated after WWI. What would stop evil men from rising up again—maybe here, in America? Margaret does not quite understand my concern, but she

*stands by me. I know what has to be done. I'm determined to fix up
the lodge and make it a place where my family can once again
protect those in need, hiding them in plain sight, just like my great-
grandaddy did for the slaves.*

So, the fifth James must have been the one who added the
locked room—not to hold someone as a prisoner, but to protect
them. Satisfaction stirs within me as all the pieces come together.

I eagerly read the last entry.

*Margaret and little James are gone. They were all I ever needed
or wanted. I regret not telling them that more often. I see no place in
this world without them and long for the day the good Lord will
take me to be with them once again.*

I don't realize I'm crying until Reid reaches out and wipes my
cheek.

Embarrassed, I let out a little laugh and swipe away the rest of
my tears. "Sorry. It's just so sad. He had good intentions but was
overwhelmed by what he'd experienced."

Reid nods. "Too bad he couldn't appreciate all he had before
it was too late."

Can a lesson be learned from the O'Malley family? Maybe
there's a reason I've felt such a strong kinship with them. Like
them, I found out the hard way how easy it is to take your blessings for granted. Hopefully, my story won't end so tragically.

~

Later that evening, Reid holds open the door of his church for
me. I enter, excited to see Josie and Liz again. Maybe I'll take them
up on their invitation to start attending youth group meetings on
a regular basis. Although, surprisingly enough, I *will* miss the little
church in Hermann.

I recognize a few familiar faces as people come up to say hello,
but I don't remember their names. Of course, I only met them
briefly at the skating party. But truth be told, I never thought I'd
see any of them again, so I didn't really pay attention when they
were introduced.

Then my gaze lands on Ryan and Cole as they approach us.
Finally, people I *do* remember.

"Hey, Emerson, nice to see you," Cole says in greeting.

"Wow." Ryan offers a sad shake of his head. "You must really be bored if you're coming to a youth group talent show."

I smile. "How could I miss a chance to see Josie and Liz perform?"

Ryan gives a lopsided grin. "I hope you enjoy musical theater because, in case you weren't aware, you will now be expected to attend every performance."

"Thanks for the warning."

Cole slaps Reid's shoulder. "Watch out, my friend. You will probably be dragged in as well."

"Em!" I turn to see Josie rushing toward me, with Liz close behind. Josie wraps me in a hug. "We're so glad you could make it."

"Of course, I wouldn't have missed it," I assure her.

Once Josie releases me, Liz takes my hand and pulls me away from the guys. "Josie and I want to give you something."

"I'm pretty sure protocol calls for the audience members to bring a gift to the performer, not the other way around," I tell her.

Liz waves off my comment, and when we reach a quiet corner, she releases my hand. "First of all, if you're able, we'd love you and Reid to join us—along with Ryan and Cole, of course—after the show for some dessert or something."

"That would be fun. We'll see what time it ends, but I can check with my dad."

"Excellent," Josie says. "But just in case it doesn't work out, we wanted to chat with you for just a few minutes."

"Oh. Okay." My caution warning lights go off.

Josie must notice something in my expression because she laughs and reaches out to touch my arm. "Don't worry. It's nothing serious."

Liz pulls out a small blue envelope from one of her sweater pockets. "We don't know what's going on in your life, but it seems like you've had a difficult time lately."

I shift with unease, hoping they don't want an explanation I can't provide.

Josie nods. "We've both faced challenges as well." She also pulls out a small envelope. Hers is lavender, with a hand-drawn heart on the front. "We just wanted to let you know that we care, and we're here for you."

"And we wanted to share some reassuring words that helped us."

I take both envelopes and stick them in the pocket of my coat. "Um, thanks. That's sweet." Before I can say anything more, I'm engulfed in a three-way hug—just like my sisters and I used to do.

Uncomfortable at first, I relax and embrace the moment of friendship.

Liz pulls away first and latches onto Josie's arm. "We should get backstage." She smiles at me. "Hopefully, we'll see you later, Em."

"Absolutely," I tell them. "Break a leg."

Liz shakes her head. "We try to avoid that saying because with Josie, you just never know."

Josie swats her friend. "Hey! I resen…okay, you're right. I resemble that."

We share a laugh, and then they disappear.

I rejoin the guys, and we chat for a few minutes before making our way into the attached school and a large open room with a stage. The space probably doubles as the school's lunchroom. There are about ten rows of chairs.

Reid drops some money in a basket and snags two cups of lemonade, while I grab a large bag of popcorn. We stop halfway down the makeshift auditorium aisle and take two chairs at the end of the row.

The youth group director leads us in prayer, and the show commences. We are entertained by a magician, a boy who plays the violin, and a girl and her dog. While the routine is clever, they don't hold a candle to Raina and Zuri. Finally, Liz and Josie take to the stage. Distracted from scanning the audience, Josie bumps into Liz, who barely seems to notice. The best friends perch on stools and sing a medley of songs from *The Sound of Music*.

Liz's crystal-clear voice holds the last note of *The Lonely Goatherd* as Josie begins to sing *DoReMi*. The song takes me back to Mrs. Clark's music class. The song she'd written especially for our class was set to this tune. The usual twinge of sadness seeps in as I think of her knack for putting unique messages into songs— little class jokes, or funny things about her beloved students.

I suddenly sit up straighter, feeling light-headed. *Could it be?*

Reid glances at me. "Are you all right?" he whispers.

I clutch his arm. "I just thought of something."

He immediately understands and nods.

Liz and Josie finish their set with a beautiful rendition of *Edelweiss*, and we join in the applause.

Reid leans close to me. "Come on, let's get out of here."

We gather our things and scurry from the room. Hopefully, my new friends won't mind our early departure.

In the lobby, we toss our trash in the garbage can.

"Shall we head for home?" Reid asks as he slips on his coat.

I shake my head. "No. Can we go somewhere to talk? I don't know if what I'm thinking makes total sense. Maybe we could puzzle it out together?"

He reaches for my hand. "I know just the place."

Fifteen minutes later, we're at a cozy coffee shop nestled in front of a fireplace, drinks in hand. A college-age girl in a long, flowy skirt sits on a small stage, singing and playing a guitar—just the noise and distraction that will allow us to speak freely.

"Okay," Reid begins. "Did you remember something else from that night?"

I shake my head. "Not exactly. But when Josie was singing *DoReMi*, and how the notes can be words, I remembered Mrs. Clark used to compose these little songs for each class."

"You think she wrote a song about whatever her husband was involved in?"

"I don't know. But the way she was moving her fingers like she was typing, it suddenly hit me, that is the same motion as playing the piano. Do you think there could be a way to put a code into a song? Similar to how James O'Malley left his coded message?"

His forehead creases as he considers my suggestion. "You're thinking that each note corresponds to a different letter?"

I nod, not sure it sounds as plausible as it did in my head a few minutes ago.

He pulls out his phone and starts surfing the internet. Soon, his eyes light up.

"You're right. It's called musical cryptography." He moves his chair close to mine so he can show me the article. His warmth and woodsy scent calm my nerves.

Shoulder to shoulder, we read how secret messages have been hidden in music for centuries. Certain notes or patterns can match up with all twenty-six letters of the alphabet. Once you have the key, you can decipher a message. The most famous example was from Johannes Brahms, who wove a love note into one of his compositions. The article even referenced a music cipher that had been created by composer Franz Josef Haydn's brother, Michael.

When finished reading, we face each other. We'd leaned so close to one another that our noses bump.

I let out a nervous laugh, while Reid smiles and leans back.

"Do you think it could be possible that Mrs. Clark hid a message in a song she wrote?" I ask, truly not sure if it makes any sense.

He rubs the back of his neck. "I don't know. It does seem a little far-fetched, but it would explain the motion she was making with her hands. And if she was a musician, especially a composer, she might have heard of hiding a message in music where no one but the intended recipient would look for it."

"Hidden in plain sight."

He lets out a low whistle. "I guess we'd better get you home so you can tell your dad."

I nod but then place my hand on his. "Or we could stay and enjoy this moment a little while longer?"

Reid holds my gaze, and I'm tempted to look away. I'm finding it harder and harder to resist his charms and that's a problem. If this theory could really crack the case, then my family would finally be safe and reunited, which would mean Dad and I could be swept away at any minute. While being with my family is all I've wanted for months, I'd be leaving a part of my heart here in Minnesota.

Chapter 20

"Hey, kid." Dad enters the room through the back door the next day. He's been working on the lodge all morning.

At the kitchen table, I close my laptop. While I'm relieved to be done with schoolwork for the day, my stomach clenches at his appearance. He was asleep when I got home last night, and he left the cabin early this morning, so I haven't yet had a chance to talk to him about the possible message in a song.

A few weeks ago, I'd have woken him up if I'd had an inkling of a lead. Now, a heavy weight of reluctance sits in the pit of my stomach. But despite my fear of leaving Minnesota and Reid, I can't keep this theory to myself. Now is probably the time to share it.

"You finished for the day already?" Will he think I'm crazy? Maybe I am.

Dad reaches into the fridge and grabs a bottle of water. "Nah. Mitch and I got a lead on an old lodge in Lake City that's closing down. The owners are selling all of their outdoor furniture. We're going to drive over and take a look."

"You and Reid's dad on a shopping spree—that sounds dangerous." I tease him, glad for the momentary reprieve from telling him about the musical code idea. "I remember the extra stuff you brought home after your last excursion."

He bends to kiss my forehead. "Okay, see you in a few hours."

"Not if I see you first."

He musses my hair and then heads back out the kitchen door. Zuri whines as he leaves and looks up at me with her big, dark eyes.

"You need to go out?" Her entire body wiggles in reply.

I let her out the back door then walk the short distance to the living room, letting her enjoy her favorite activity: circling the cabin, sniffing out every tree, and making sure all is well before ending up on the front porch. As I wait on the living room sofa for her return, I watch Mr. Stevenson climb into Dad's truck, and then follow its path out toward the road.

Even though they're technically employer and employee, it looks like they've become good friends. I'm glad Dad has made a friend—one who also knows our situation. Uprooting his whole life and being separated from his wife and younger daughters can't be easy. For too long, I've focused only on my feelings, not on how the situation has affected everyone else. Time for that to change. Maybe I can do something special for Dad. Or at least go ahead and tell him my theory about the music message. After all, the only thing he really wants is for our family to be reunited. No more putting it off. Tonight, I'll tell him.

Deciding to join Zuri outside, I pull on my coat, hat, and boots. She bounces with excitement until I hold up her booties. Obediently, she remains still so I can put them on her. Today, we venture down the path to the lake. I brush snow off one of the benches at the gazebo and take a seat, peering out at the pristine, frozen lake, the evergreens dusted with snow, and the puffy white clouds gliding across the blue sky.

Off to the right, Mrs. Stevenson backs her car out of their garage and follows the path Dad's pickup took to the main road, presumably on her way to pick up Raina from school. Reid told me last night that he had a meeting after school regarding the upcoming pre-season workouts for track and field, so he won't be doing the whole Driving-Miss-Raina routine today. That means I have a few more hours to myself.

I lean back and shove my hands in my pockets, discovering the notes from Liz and Josie. I'd forgotten all about them after my unexpected realization regarding Mrs. Clark.

My gloves make it difficult, but with enough fumbling, I'm able to open the light blue envelope and pull out a folded note card. Inside is a handwritten message from Liz and a prayer card with a picture of a religious sister wearing a black habit. I start with the letter.

Emerson,

Someday, I'll share with you everything that happened on the recent cruise I took with my dad. But since that experience, I decided to look closely at the Catholic Faith. I started with a book about some amazing Catholics. There was one that I connected with—Blessed Julia Rodzinska. She was a sister who ran an orphanage in Poland during World War II. Sr. Julia was arrested by the Nazis and placed in solitary confinement. For a year, she was alone in a tiny, cement room before they sent her to a concentration camp. She must have felt so alone and abandoned. But instead of turning away from God during her trials, she turned toward Him, even teaching other prisoners to pray the Rosary.

For years, I've had a rocky relationship with my dad, and I held on to so much pain and anger for way too long. I'm still working on it, but reading about Sr. Julia helped me understand that there are people with far greater problems than mine, and they have been able to endure through God's strength. The various stories somehow helped me feel less alone. You don't need to feel that way, either. If you ever feel like talking, Josie and I are here for you. In the meantime, I'll be praying for you.

Liz

I fold the note, return it to its envelope, and open Josie's. Her note is accompanied by a quote and a Bible verse.

I sure hope you don't mind us trying to help. We've enjoyed getting to know you and just want you to be happy. Whatever challenges are in your life, please be assured that God cares for you. Sometimes, it's hard to see and believe, but it's true. Last summer, when I was going through a tough time, my mom kept sending me Bible verses. At first, I was annoyed, but then the words began to speak to me. The one that resonated the most was Psalm 27:1—The Lord is my light and my salvation. Whom shall I fear? The Lord is the strength of my life. Of whom shall I be afraid?

And I recently found this quote from St. Ignatius:
    "If God sends you many sufferings, it is a sign that He has great plans for you and certainly wants to make you a saint."
    I keep it by my bed so I won't forget that I'm not the only one who suffers. Knowing God has plans for each of us, plans that can sometimes only come about through difficulties, has been a comfort to me.
    I think God has some amazing things planned for you, too.

Your friend, Josie

I press the notes against my chest. My heart was as cold as a Minnesota winter when I first arrived here. I was trying to shut God out. Logically, I knew He wasn't to blame, but my heart wasn't so sure. He could've prevented everything from happening, but He didn't. My unanswered prayers seemed proof that my life didn't matter.

But maybe Reid was right. God was watching over me the whole time and I was too blind to see it. After all, He had protected us and kept us all safe. Hopefully, in His timing, we will be reunited someday.

I bow my head and close my eyes.

God, thank you for bringing these amazing friends into my life when I needed them most. I'm so sorry I doubted Your love and tried to push You away. You are exactly what I need. My life may never be normal again, but I can see now that I'm stronger for what I've been through, and You've been with me every step of the way—protecting me, guiding me, and maybe even helping me to be the person who can bring justice to the Clarks. Please keep guiding my steps. I love You.

My phone buzzes. It's a message from Reid with a link to a podcast about musical cryptography. Guess he couldn't get the idea out of his mind, either. I've been waffling between "it makes total sense" and "what an absurd idea." Knowing Reid thinks there is some merit to the theory is comforting. But what will Dad think?

As I head back to the cabin with Zuri, another idea sparks. To make up for being such a lousy roommate, I should make a special dinner—even if it is just one of Mrs. Stevenson's creations, before I start the tidying up process.

Maybe the podcast will help me figure out how to broach the subject. Before I get started, I insert my earbuds and click on the link Reid sent. While the sink fills with warm, bubbly water, I twist my hair up in a messy bun and secure it with a barrette. The show begins with an introduction of the podcast hosts, two friends who are obsessed with unusual crimes. After a few minutes of bantering back and forth, they finally begin discussing the issue.

I'm totally immersed in the episode and the fascinating case about a musical cypher when Zuri's barking pulls me from the show. I look over my shoulder at my frenzied dog. Her ears are flat against her head as she ferociously barks at the back door from a crouched position. I grab a dish towel to dry my hands, then pause the episode. As I yank the earbuds from my ears, I wonder what has Zuri so agitated. A wild animal?

Please, God, not a bear.

Almost before the thought is complete, the back door bursts open with a deafening boom and crashes into the wall. Splintered wood from the shattered door frame flies across the room with fierce velocity. I have no time to react or understand what is happening.

A huge man steps into the ruined doorway. His dark eyes zero in on me, and an evil sneer pulls his lips into something far, far from a smile. Ice-cold fear instantly clutches me. His is a face I'll never forget from all those months ago, inside the Carters' house, where he stood as a menacing guard over their meeting.

My heart races, while my feet remain frozen in place. This scenario has replayed in my nightmares for months. I can't believe it is now unfolding in front of me. How did they find us?

Zuri continues her manic barking.

"Shut your dog up, or I will." His threatening tone fills me with fear.

I back up against the counter, panic stealing my ability to think. All I can do is stare at the monster inside our kitchen.

The man takes a step forward, and Zuri lunges at him. With an explosive kick, he sends her skidding across the hardwood floor. Her body slams into the wall with a sickening thud. Then he reaches behind his back and pulls a gun from his waistband. He points it at her.

"No!" I scream.

Zuri whimpers, looking at me with sad eyes that break my heart. Her head sags to the floor, and she stops moving.

The blood seems to drain from my body as I stare at my injured dog, willing her to be okay. I inch my hand toward my phone, on the counter beside the sink. We need help.

Satisfied that my precious dog is no longer a threat, the man aims his attention and the gun toward me. He glances at my hand and slowly shakes his head. In two quick steps, he's inches from me. My terror and the stench of his stale breath make me gag. I struggle to keep my lunch from resurfacing.

"Don't think so, sweetheart." With one swift move, he crushes my phone beneath the grip of his gun. Then he yanks my arm with incredible force, clearly enjoying himself. Fire rips upward from elbow to shoulder and makes a lightning-quick swoop down into my shoulder blade. I can't bite back an agonized yelp.

His lips thin in satisfaction. "You're coming with me, missy."

Grasping for some way to slow things down, I nod. "Fine," I grit through clenched teeth, determined to show him no further reaction. "I need shoes, though."

His gaze flicks to my stockinged feet and he lets out a disgusted grunt.

"My boots and jacket are by the front door." My mind races for a way to escape.

He shoves me toward the living room and releases my arm, but the gun remains pointed at me.

Keeping an eye on him, I slowly walk to the front door and slip into my boots. *Now what?* How do I get away? I'm reaching for my jacket when I see movement behind his bulk. Zuri. My heart fills with relief. She's okay. She was just playing dead, as Raina taught her.

My brief thanksgiving is replaced with a new wave of terror, as I realize what my Zuri is doing.

Oh, no. No, no, no. I silently beg her to stop as she stealthily sneaks up on her prey. *Please don't try to help.* I silently plead with her. *He'll kill you.* But when she leaps, she's transformed from my sweet, lovable canine pal into a vicious, wild animal. The man must notice my gaze, because he turns toward what has captured my attention just as Zuri reaches him, barreling through the air as if on wings. Her bared teeth sink into the closest target—the hand that holds the gun—forcing the intruder to drop it.

Without hesitation, I kick the deadly weapon, and it skids across the wooden floor and into my bedroom. Every fiber of my being wants to stay and make sure my beloved pet is all right, but logic kicks in. She's risked her life to give me a chance to escape. Without taking time to even grab my coat, I fly out the door and sprint as fast as I can toward the lodge. The last thing I hear is Zuri's squeal of pain. Tears stream down my face. *Oh, Zur, I'm so sorry.*

I force my legs to keep moving away from her. The man can easily overtake me, but maybe the few moments he'll spend searching for his gun will provide the time I need to reach the lodge and get inside one of the hidden rooms.

My lungs burn from exertion and the bitter cold as I will myself to run across the snow, faster than I've ever moved before. I don't risk taking the time to look back.

Please, God, be with me. Guardian angel, help me.

I reach the side door in record time, yank it open, and sprint down the hallway. The stairs come into view, but taking them will slow me down. Better to get to the hidden room beside the library. I'm rounding the corner when the side door slams open, crashing into the wall.

"There's no sense in hiding!" The booming voice reverberates through the lodge, increasing my fear and my speed.

Once I reach the library, the carpet muffles my footsteps. I dash toward the wall with the hidden door.

"I will find you, missy. My orders are to *try* to bring you in alive, but I'm sure my employers will understand that it just wasn't possible. They never said anything about roughing you up a bit, either. Making me angry is not a wise move."

I press on the door as gently as possible, hoping to avoid making any sound. Only a slight creak accompanies the sliding wood door. I slip into the billiard room and hold my breath as I gently close the door. Then I lean against the wall beside it and breathe a sigh of relief. I'm safe. But now what? Do I stay hidden and wait for him to leave? Will he? Or will he keep searching? Reid's mom and Raina will probably return before Dad and Mr. Stevenson.

What would this monster do to them? Or to Dad when he returns? I can't allow this man to hurt anyone else.

If only I could capture him somehow. My mind whirls with possibilities. A plausible scenario comes to mind.

I squeeze my eyes shut. *Please, Lord, help me. I trust in You.*

Thinking through each step of my plan, I decide it's worth a try. Unfortunately, the first step involves getting to the other side of the lodge to access the other hidden rooms. Since Reid and I never found a passage connecting them, there are only two ways—via the kitchen pantry, or through the upstairs hallway. With the henchman almost certainly searching this level first, I'll need to go with option two.

With forced confidence, I push off from the wall and open the hidden passageway Zuri and I discovered that leads to the staircase on this side of the lodge. I have no idea how soundproof these rooms are, so I tread lightly up the winding staircase. Before entering the upstairs closet, I pause, tuned in to every nuance of sound. Hearing nothing, I gently push open the door and inch into the closet. With a deep breath, I open the hidden panel of the wardrobe and slip into the bedroom.

My pursuer's muffled voice breaks the silence. "All I need is to know what you remembered." The sound of furniture being shoved aside wafts up to me.

Sounds like he's still downstairs. I slink out of the room and silently pad down the long hallway toward the bedroom on the other end.

"I'd sure hate to start looking for your mom and sisters."

His threat briefly halts me. So much for separating us to protect us. I force myself to continue moving.

"My client's power is far-reaching. None of you will ever be safe."

His voice is clearer now, and soon, I hear him coming up the main staircase.

I silently dash into the far bedroom and rush to the hidden compartment. Once the panel is open, I slither through the opening and slide the door shut behind me. After a few breaths to calm my nerves, I head down the spiral staircase, past the kitchen supply closet, and all the way to the basement.

The little chapel area is once again bathed in a green glow from the high window. Before moving on to the next part of my plan, I kneel in front of the crucifix.

Lord, please keep me safe. Guide my steps and please be with me always. I'm sorry I thought I didn't need You. I was wrong. I will always need You.

I make the sign of the cross, then push myself to my feet and move on to the small bedroom. On my way to the tunnel entrance, I stop before the picture of James O'Malley V. While it's not exactly what he had in mind, his hidden rooms may just keep a family safe after all.

Thank you.

After several shoves, I'm able to push the heavy dresser in front of the tunnel door that leads to the tiny cabin Reid and I reached by snowshoe. Hopefully this will keep it from opening. Exhausted, I lean against it. Now for the tricky part.

I pass back through the chapel and go up one flight of stairs to reach the kitchen's supply closet. Cracking open the door, I listen for the hunter. It's not hard to determine his location. Despite the distance, I can hear he's upstairs, hurling threats and furniture as he continues a single-minded search for his prey—me.

I start to silently chant. *This will work. This will work.*

Feigning bravery, I force myself to leave the kitchen through the swinging doors. I run through the dining room and push open the glass doors that lead to the back deck. Taking the porch steps two at a time, I sprint toward the lake. My focus lasers in on the woods and the general direction of the little cabin—which suddenly feels too far away. Is it even possible to make it there from here? How will I know when I've gone far enough? Is the lake even solid all the way out there? In this bitter cold, of course it is.

With only one way to find out, I take a step onto the lake. My foot slips along the still surface. Ice skates sure would come in handy right now. And a coat. And gloves. I push away from the dock, shuffling and sliding along the ice, hoping for once that he sees me since my plan depends on it. I shove my hands in my armpits to warm them but without my outstretched arms to keep me steady, my progress slows, so I abandon the warming idea.

I've only covered a few yards when an explosive blast startles me, knocking me off my feet. I hit the ice hard. *What was that?*

I glance back to see my nemesis standing on the patio, his extended hands wrapped around his gun.

He's shooting at me? I hadn't expected that. Didn't he say he wanted me alive?

I scramble to my feet, my hands achingly cold as I push myself off the ice. Another blast sounds as a bullet ricochets off the ice and skims along the frozen surface. Realization hits in a horrid flash. He's not trying to shoot me. Surely a bodyguard would have better aim than that. His orders were to bring me in alive. He's trying to break the ice. Falling into the lake would be just as fatal as a bullet but could be played off as an accident. I scramble toward the shore. I'll need to travel the rest of the way through the woods.

Every inch of me screams as I claw my way off the lake and over a snowbank. My fingers throb from the cold, my arm and shoulder still burn from his initial attack, my hips aches from my fall, and my lungs burn as I gasp in the frigid air. Each anguished movement causes me to sink into the snow, but eventually, I manage to shimmy and slide off the tall bank, landing with a jarring jolt on the makeshift path Reid and I created days earlier.

Afraid I'll never get up if I rest for even a moment, I struggle to my feet and keep moving. Despite the matted-down snow, plodding forward without snowshoes is tedious as I sink nearly to my knees with each step. At least laboring through the deep snow warms me up, except for my hands. I cup them around my mouth and blow on them without breaking my stride.

Behind me, the man's curses echo through the valley as he follows me across the lake. His fury urges me on, but in trying to hurry, I stumble and pitch forward. Instinctively, I try to brace my fall but only sink into the thick white powder. My face follows suit. *Keep moving!*

I manage to sit back into one of my footprints and take a moment to scan the woods—the little cabin finally is in view. Tears sting my eyes as I behold the most welcoming sight I may ever have seen. Drawing on my last reserve of energy, I force my uncooperative legs to keep moving. *Come on, you've got this.*

I reach the cabin and kick the snowdrifts away from the door. Precious moments are wasted fumbling with the latch, but finally the door swings open. I stumble inside, knowing I don't have much time. My pursuer could be here any minute.

Looking in the direction of the hidden door, my heart sinks. I'd hoped that the heavy chest was still where Reid had moved it, but he must have come back and replaced it. Tears of frustration sting my eyes but I can't give up. With hands that are practically useless, I sit with my back to the wooden wall and, using my legs, shove the heavy chest away from the hidden compartment. I try to pry open the floorboard with my fingers, but the slit is so thin, the attempt would be futile. Panic surges through me as I wonder how much time I have before he finds me. Each moment that ticks away decreases my chances of success. I scan the room for a rusty nail or piece of wood, but there's nothing.

Think! You can't give up now.

Frustrated, I lean my head back against the rough wooden wall behind me. That's when I feel the barrette that's holding back my hair. *Yes!* Numb fingers make the simple task of unclasping the metal a challenge. At last, after three frustrating failures, it springs opens.

My hair tumbles over my shoulders as I wedge the metal piece of the barrette between two of the floorboards. As I work, the man's threats and curses grow louder.

Hurry!

The barrette slips from my grasp, but I'm able to catch it before it hits the floor. I wedge it between the floorboards again and apply some pressure. The trapdoor lifts just enough that I'm able to pull it open. I slip inside the dark cellar and army-crawl into the dark recesses of storage space. Behind an abandoned crate, I slither under an old musty-smelling tarp. Desperate to create a little warmth, I pull my sweater over my nose, curl into a little ball, and retract my hands inside my sleeves.

Before long, the cabin door bangs open and heavy footsteps cross the floor.

"You are a piece of work, you know that? You will pay for this." Each word drips with venom.

I hold my breath when the hunter steps into the storage space, so close I could reach out and touch his leg. The flashlight from his phone turns on, and I'm sure it's all over. *Please, Lord, keep me safe.* I squeeze my eyes shut as the light comes my way. Instead of checking behind the old crates, though, I hear him continue down into the tunnel.

I open my eyes and let out a slow, silent breath. *Thank you, Lord.*

All I want is for this nightmare to be over, but I have to leave my safe haven in order for that to happen. After the man's footsteps have receded, I force my aching limbs to move and crawl out of the space—each inch a struggle.

Come on, you can do this.

I manage to pull myself out of the hole in the floor. With fingers that refuse to cooperate, I shut the trap door then work on trying to push the chest back into place. But I'm so tired and cold, I can barely move.

A hand touches my shoulder.

"No!" I shriek and fly out from under the hand, my feet backpeddling against the floor as I try to scramble away.

"Em!"

Finally, I focus on the face hovering above me: Reid. That's when the tears begin to flow.

"It's okay." He glances at the half-covered cellar door. "Is he down there?"

I nod. "It's the D.A.'s bodyguard. I blocked the door at the end of the tunnel, then lured him here. He's trapped."

Reid's eyebrows raise in what appears to be admiration. "Well done." With one quick shove, he finishes pushing the chest over the trapdoor, then kneels and wraps his arms around me. "I'm so sorry if our search led him to you. But you're safe now."

His warm presence is overwhelming, and uncontrollable sobs shake my entire body. He rubs my back, patiently waiting until I'm able to speak.

"How did you know where I was?" I manage the words between gasps of breath. My shaking, numb fingers attempt to wipe away the tears.

Looking at the odd, blue color of my hands, he winces. "Oh, Em. Here." He pulls off his gloves and slides them on my hands before explaining. "When I pulled into the lane, Zuri was sitting in the middle of the road."

"She's alive?" Intense relief floods me, and fresh tears spill from my eyes.

He nods. "But I immediately knew something was wrong. I stopped and opened my door, but she wouldn't get in. Instead, she began limping away, like she was leading me. I followed along in my car, and when I saw that the front door to the cabin was wide open, I knew you were in trouble. That's when I heard the blast and saw you on the ice." He pulls off his coat and wraps it around me. "I've never been so scared."

"Is everyone else safe? I was so afraid if anyone came home, he'd hurt them." Chattering teeth make it difficult to speak.

"Everyone is fine, except…well, I couldn't get Zuri into my house, and didn't want her trying to go after you, so I lifted her and put her in my car." That grin that I've come to adore makes a welcome appearance. "She was so frantic to protect you, I wouldn't be surprised if she tears the upholstery to shreds trying to escape."

My eyes tear up again as I think of my brave, sweet pup.

He pulls me further into his warmth. "While following your tracks in the snow, I called my dad and John, his marshal friend. They should be here any moment."

With the faint sound of sirens in the distance, I finally relax against him.

I'm safe.

Epilogue

Several Months Later

I lean my head against Reid's shoulder as we sit on the dock, dipping our feet into the lake. Zuri sits on my other side, watching the ducks paddling across the lake. The last few months have brought more changes than just the warmer weather. We've grown quite close, and my faith has been restored. And maybe the most exciting change is about to happen.

"Are you nervous about seeing them?" Reid rests his head on mine.

I swirl my toes through the water, creating a little wake. "Yes. I can't control the fluttering in my stomach."

At long last, my family will be reunited. Reid's parents graciously offered the nearly renovated lodge for the reunion. Hard to believe my grandparents, aunt, uncle, cousins, sisters, parents, and I will soon be together at the lodge—a whole week together as we try to sort out all that has transpired and what the future will hold. I can't wait to show my sisters and cousins the secret passageways, but I'm especially excited to introduce them to Reid, who has truly been a godsend.

The two of us have become even closer over the last few months as my family sorted through the legal issues. Thanks to our theory about the hidden musical code and the countless hours the agents spent deciphering the musical scores that Mrs. Clark had written, the FBI finally had the proof they needed. The ring of crime was far-reaching and involved politicians, policemen, judges, lawyers, and businessmen in numerous states. Completely unraveling the tangled web of deceit could take years—that, and holding everyone accountable for their long list of crimes—racketeering, theft, drug-related charges, kidnapping, money laundering, and even murder.

We are now free to return to our lives and our real identities. That is, if we want to. A lot of discussion has already taken place between us about that. Do we want to open ourselves up to the scrutiny of the press and the likely anger of some people whose lives are now ruined? With their family members involved in illegal activities, innocent family members have had their lives turned upside down. Not everyone will welcome us back in our hometown.

Turns out, Mom and the girls have been in Washington state, and have no desire to stay there. My grandparents have been living in Louisiana. They liked it there, but of course they want to be reunited with us. Keira and her family were in Vermont, but long to return to the Midwest. I plan on pleading my case that they all consider permanently relocating here. Once you get used to the winters, it's a pretty amazing place to live.

Keira and I have been able to chat on the phone—for hours. I've told her all about Reid, and we finally had a chance to discuss all that we'd witnessed. She really had been our *39 Steps* messenger. Our parents couldn't believe we'd been able to find each other and provide the needed details to solve the case.

"So, have you given any thought to what name you're going to use?" Reid asks me. "Calling you anything other than Emerson will take some getting used to. I see why the marshals had you choose similar names, such as Emma or Emily."

I sit up. "Actually, my real name doesn't start with an *E*—it starts with an *M*."

He jolts, his surprise obvious. Then he grins as he catches on. "Of course! Em, El, and Es are actually the letters *M*, *L*, and *S*."

I laugh. "Yep. But don't panic yet. That's something else my family needs to discuss. If we're starting over, maybe keeping our new names isn't such a bad idea."

"Well, you'll need to figure out a name for the byline of your article."

I smile, thinking of the project that has kept me busy while the legal system sorted out our case. "I'm so happy Mrs. Grier encouraged me to share the truth about the O'Malley family. And I still can't believe Josie's mom connected me with that magazine editor."

"It's helpful to have connections with a local author," Reid agrees.

"It's nice that the article will come out right before the lodge's grand opening event. Hopefully, the historical details will intrigue a lot of people who will want to visit and book some family trips."

Reid chuckles. "Mom's initial excitement about the timing of the article has been replaced with anxiety. Now that her dream is becoming a reality, she's kinda freaking out."

"Well, my family's week here will be a good test run before the place opens for the public."

"Good point. I'll make sure to remind her of that."

I stare out at the beautiful lake and surrounding trees. "You know, I think James O'Malley V would be happy to know that his family name will finally be cleared." I stroke Zuri's back, so thankful for her loyalty and that we both recovered from our ordeal.

"I think so, too." Reid pulls me in for a hug. "Have I told you yet today how amazing you are? You've been through so much and never gave up. I think you're pretty inspiring."

I snuggle into him again. "You have no idea how much you helped me these last few months. I was so sad when we first moved here. You were the one who made it clear that my life wasn't over and that I should rely on God."

We're quiet for a moment, and then he runs his fingers through my hair. "Do you think your mom will like me?"

A glint of light catches my eye, and I look toward the lane. Butterflies tumble inside me. "Guess we'll find out in a few minutes. Looks like they're here." Dust kicks up as two dark SUVs slowly enter the property.

Reid stands and helps me to my feet. He draws me in for one more hug, then lowers his head and gently touches his lips to mine in a brief-but-oh-so-sweet kiss. Our first. Then, while my heart still pounds and my tummy flutters with an entire kaleidoscope of butterflies, he turns and starts to lead me away to greet my family.

I lift my hand. "Give me a moment, okay?"

He nods and, somehow understanding my request, walks toward the lodge without a word. Zuri watches me for a moment then trots after him.

I take a moment to look out over the clear water of the lake that I've come to love. My gaze moves to the woods where I had to flee for my life. God was always here, right in front of me, in plain sight. I just needed to find enough faith to truly believe it.

Thank You, God, for being patient with me. I know that life will continue to throw challenges my way, but I promise to always trust in You.

I turn and walk slowly toward the group of people clustered around the newly arrived SUVs. But my pace rapidly increases, and soon I break into a run, because they're all waiting. My new friends. My family. And whatever comes next for all of us.

Acknowledgements

There are a few people I'd like to thank for helping get this novel published.

To God, for leading me down this writing pathway.

My husband, for his unwavering support in every venture I try.

The Mental family, for giving me so many moments of joy and inspiration.

Tressa Lindsay of Bird's Eye Edits, for making the story shine and dealing with all those punctuation nuisances.

My author friends at CatholicTeenBooks, who have become much more than coworkers.

Janet Johnson, Amanda Lauer, and Andrea Jo Rodgers for providing valuable feedback.

Perpetual Light Publishing, for giving this series a new home.

To the loyal readers who provided ideas for character names which sparked new ideas for the story, especially Brianna Zonneveld, Emily R. McCormick, Emma, Amanda, and Gianna.

And to all the readers, thank you for taking the time to read this book.

If you enjoyed the story, please take a moment to post a review or share with a friend.

To M,

From the excitement of D.C. and the beauty of Minnesota to the glorious mountains of Colorado and our awe-inspiring travels, thanks for this amazing life of adventure.

L

Reader Guide/Questions

1) Emerson loves to read. She especially enjoys the classics. Do you have a favorite book or author? Do you prefer contemporary stories or classics? Why?

2) Emerson and Reid become intrigued by the mysterious history of the lodge. Have you ever researched the history of a place you enjoy? Does your home have an interesting background?

3) Emerson is warmly welcomed by Josie and Liz. Was there ever a time when people welcomed you in a new situation? Or have you experienced a time when people were not so welcoming? Do you try to be someone who reaches out to newcomers?

4) Josie and Liz recognized that Emerson was going through a rough time and offered her prayers and encouragement. While expressing our faith is difficult, it can be exactly the light someone needs. Why is it so challenging to share our beliefs with others? (If you are curious about the backstories of Josie and Liz, you can check out the previous two books in my Finding Faith series, Into the Spotlight and Charting the Course.)

5) Emerson believes her prayers are not being answered. Have you ever felt that way? How did you handle those feelings?

6) Do you trust God completely with your life? Do you try to solve your own problems before you give them to God in prayer?

7) When Emerson and her cousin shared what they knew about a dangerous situation, their families were put in danger. Do you think it was the right decision?

8) Emerson regrets taking her previous life for granted. If everything you knew suddenly changed, how would you feel? Take a moment to reflect on all the good things in your life.

9) The internet can be an amazing tool, but it can also cause problems, such as leading us to harmful sites, exposing us to things shouldn't be viewing, and inviting us into interactions

with dangerous people. Do you think it's wise for parents to limit internet activity?

10) If you were part of Emerson's family, would you want to create a new home in Minnesota or go back home to Missouri? What are the pros and cons of each scenario?